BE MY VALERIE!

PASSPORT TO LOVE SERIES

ANNA FOXKIRK

Be My Valerie! Copyright © 2021 by Anna Foxkirk

All rights reserved.

Second edition of Be My Valerie! published in 2023.

No part of this book may be reproduced in any form or by any electronic or mechanical means, including information storage and retrieval systems, without written permission from the author, except for the use of brief quotations in a book review.

This book is a work of fiction. All characters and events in this publication, other than those clearly in the public domain are fictitious and any resemblance to real persons living or dead, is purely coincidental.

Please note that although Anna Foxkirk is an Australian author, American English has been used in this novel.

❀ Created with Vellum

FOREWORD

Thanks for choosing to read *Be My Valerie*. I hope you have as much fun reading this as I had writing it. It gives you a taste of my *Passport to Love* series. If you want to be the first to learn about upcoming releases, please sign up to my newsletter. If you want to make my 'happy ever after' please don't forget to leave a review!

Although *Be My Valerie* is an imagined story, in part at least, it is inspired by my previous skiing holidays in the French Alps. I was never a chalet girl, but I've heard a few hair-raising stories...

Be My Valentine! is written for my one and only true Valentine — Steve Greene. Steve, you are my everything!

1

VALERIE

The hike from the supermarket to home is short enough not to justify hopping on the bus, but just long enough to make me wish I had: my arms are stretched out of their sockets, weighed down with bags full of groceries, and now Simon and Tracey are blocking my path — the last two people on the planet I want to run into.

My step falters, but it's too late to dart into a side alley or slink back the way I've come. Besides, the knife which has skewered my heart for the past couple of weeks, is now twisting slowly and painfully like I'm some sort of human walking kebab. It makes any rational decision-making impossible.

Should I turn around in the hope they haven't seen me? Or should I walk on by and pretend they're not even there?

Gritting my teeth, holding my breath, I manage to keep robotically putting one foot in front of the other. I imagine this must be what it feels like to walk toward your own execution. Honestly, the way they're kissing you'd think they were trying to extract one another's teeth with their tongues.

Eyes glued to the sidewalk, I squeeze past ... accidentally swiping Simon around the back of his legs with one of my shopping bags.

His knees buckle. "Bloody hell! Watch where you're going!" he says, coming up for air. "Oh, it's you."

Yes, it's me, Valerie Pickles, your hopelessly devoted reject. But I don't pause because my shopping bags are bulging with groceries and my eyes are bulging with unshed tears.

"Get a life, you stupid cow!" shouts Tracey.

"Oh piss off yourself!" I mutter. "Get a bedroom!"

Brave face fixed in place, jaw rigid and eyes smarting, I reach the end of our cul-de-sac, grateful to have made it to our weed-woven patch of front lawn and familiar porch its paint peeling like its got a bad case of sunburn.

Putting my bags down, I fumble with the keys desperate to get inside before the dam bursts and I start wailing in public. As soon as I slam the door behind me, the air whistles out of my lungs and I howl.

It's pitiful, really, crying like a baby, like this. And it's ugly. When, oh when, will I get over Simon? Will it be before I'm old and gray? Any time this century?

Thankfully, Mum, who can be overly protective, isn't home to witness my meltdown.

With about as much life as a limp lettuce, I decant the shopping into the pantry and fridge, and stumble upstairs to my bedroom. I cannot help but indulge in a bout of self-pity. How has this become my life? Last year I was so deliriously happy. Last year, Simon and I were an 'item'.

Blowing my nose, I sit at my desk, open my laptop and stare at the blank screen in front of me. My backbone sags. How the heck do I write about love when my love life is non-existent? *Blah, blah, blah,* I write, which isn't the most promising line for a great romance story. *Blah bloody blah.* Last year I was on a roll. I wrote two romance novellas, but now this — it's like the white wall of the north. A whiteout blizzard. Perhaps I need to start a new project. Or do some browsing for inspiration.

I check my Instagram, as you do, while you're contemplating your next masterful blockbusting plot. My brother Ben's feed consists of frame after frame of the usual debauched university lifestyle. Me, jealous of my brother? Hah! Why ever would I be? Gemma, my best friend from school, is having a ball in Méricoeur; skiing and drinking and — I squint at the screen — yet again entangled in some random's embrace. And of course, I can't help checking out Simon's posts. *Oh, fetch me a bucket, puh-lease*! I really wish I hadn't. There are dozens of pictures of him and Tracey mauling one another. They're disgustingly tactile and not afraid of PDLs — public displays of lust. Best put my phone down before I sink any deeper. *You'll never write a romance story if you only focus on your own failure.*

Must concentrate on happy ever after.

Must also just nip downstairs to get some chocolate to boost morale.

Back at my desk, unpeeling the wrapper, I'm distracted by the snow globe Gemma sent me for Christmas — it's a gift-giving tradition between the pair of us going back to her once accidentally breaking one of my snow globes when I was eight — along with her card instructing me to get my butt out to Méricoeur! It's good to feel wanted by someone, I guess. I'd be out there like a shot, but that's *her* adventure and I don't want to rain on her parade. And let's be honest here, you never know when Simon might see sense and realize he's made a terrible mistake. Clearly, he and Tracey are not right for each other.

I give the snow globe a shake. A dandruff of snow patters down over a couple holding hands, carrying their skis over their shoulders. I wouldn't mind being trapped in a snow globe with Simon. *Damn. Stop it!* I must stop thinking about him. It just makes me feel even more depressed. I'm becoming horribly cynical about love and happy ever afters because I'm stuck in my hometown with no escape in sight and I've turned into a sappy ever after. Leaving here would mean leaving Simon. I know the panic I feel whenever I consider that is pathetic. I know I have to do something dramatic, but it's SO. DAMN. HARD. Tracey, the cow, is right of course. I do need to get a life. But I can't seem to summon up the energy required.

As if summoned by magic and wishful thinking, my phone rings and Gemma's name pops up on the screen. I throw myself on my bed, ready to receive my fill of thrilling Alpine news about who she's out-skiing, or out-drinking or out snogging in merry old Méricoeur.

"New Year's Eve was amazing, Val! You should've seen the fireworks! They were epic! The only thing that would have made it better was having you there, at least then I wouldn't have drunk myself into a stupor."

I smile. That's my girl — party beast. "You think? Tell me what happened then." After all, I can live and love vicariously, and it's all potential fodder for my writing.

She prattles on excitedly, barely pausing for breath for another twenty minutes. *Chalet life is the best ...* I'm happy for her. Of course, I am. Not bitter at all. I give the snow globe another good shake. Gemma's bubble world is a bit different to mine: all fluffy snow and happy couples fornicating under the fireworks, skiing without breaking their necks; whereas mine is staring at the rising damp, peeling wallpaper and eating tv suppers with Mum.

"So how was your New Year's Eve?" she asks.

"Oh, fine. A bit quiet. But you know, this is Burtonbridge." I laugh, but it sounds strained.

"And did you see Slime-on?"

If she means, did I see Simon going into Tracey's house next door with his hand up her sweater, then yes, I definitely did, unfortunately. "Not really. I decided to stay in."

"Now, listen here, Val, my old mucker," she says, "what you need is to get out. And I don't mean out to the supermarket, I mean *out*, out. Out of Burtonbridge. Preferably out here. You're not sounding like yourself at all."

I steel myself for the barrage that's bound to follow. God love her.

"You need to get your head out of the clouds. Stop pining for the impossible. There's no such thing as love, not really," she informs me with her customary dose of sympathy. "It's a construct. A crutch for the weak. Simon leaving you was the best thing that could've ever happened. The bloke's a total knobhead anyhow. We both know that. I know it might feel painful at present, but being Slimed is not unlike wiping out on the piste. It's a shock, it's humiliating, but it's over. Now you need to get off your ruddy backside and back on your feet and keep skiing."

"Of course. Great analogy. The fact I don't ski is neither here nor there..." I put the snow globe down before I hurl it across my bedroom. I'm not angry with Gemma — I adore her — I'm angry with myself and what a momentous failure I am.

"There are plenty of jobs out here. What on earth are you waiting for. An avalanche to hit?" says Gemma. "Come and join me, Val. You know you want to. It's got to be better than doing nothing."

"But I'm writing," I lie.

Despite getting good grades from school, I've done nothing with them. I passed on university because I wanted to stay here with Simon. I had this romantic notion of writing my bestseller while he was working on the farm. Now I'm incapable of writing because all I can think about is Simon. Simon. Simon.

Slime-on.

I can't even speak anymore because I'm afraid that if I do my voice might crack and the trickle of tears will become a deluge.

"There's nothing to stop you writing out here and the perfect opportunity has come up." I hold it together while Gemma starts babbling on about the other girl in her chalet who's fallen off a table while dancing and broken her ankle. Amazing it wasn't Gemma.

I zone out a bit, distracted by the horrible bumping noise now coming through the bedroom wall next to me. The walls are paper thin in these terrace houses.

"You need to have a life if you want to write about life," says Gemma.

What are they doing next door? Oh. No. Ewww! It has to be Simon and Tracey. I swear it's deliberate. Not listening! Not listening! So. Not. listening! La, la, la, la, la...

"Don't you think, Valerie? Valerie!"

"Mmmm? Yes, I suppose."

"So, you'll do it?" she asks.

"Do what?"

"Have you listened to a word I've said?"

It's a bit hard, with all the bumping and furniture moving going on next door. "Of course, I have. It's just ... to be honest ... Simon and Tracey are at it again. I can hear them through the flipping wall. I never had that much sex with him!" I whisper hoarsely. "It's endless, a-and disturbing the peace, and quite frankly it's driving me nuts!" I give the wall a thump.

"Oh, Val. Forget about them and get yourself over here. I've just offered the perfect escape. If you'd been paying any attention at all what with Charlotte breaking her ankle, there's an opening here at the chalet. You'd be perfect. You're a domestic goddess. Think of all the baking you could do. And you'd have plenty of time for your writing too while everyone else is out on the pistes. Time to ring in a few changes for the new year, don't you think?"

"I'd love to but ..." It's a good thing she can't see me lying on my bed, mouth puckering and eyes scrunching up in the effort not to cry. Talk about going downhill fast. Who needs skis? Ever since Simon left me, I've been on a slippery slope. I can't sleep. I can't think. I've barely written a word. My get-up-and-go has got up and gone. If it's possible, I hate myself even more than I hate Tracey — actually, that's not possible. But anything, *anything*, would be better than listening to another bout of her high-pitched squeals and his animal grunts. Even a job in a ski resort.

"Val, what do you think?" asks Gemma.

"I think if this other girl broke her ankle, that's hardly a ringing endorsement for me to take the job on, is it? And me, a chalet girl? Get real. I can't even ski, Gem!"

"You don't have to ski. You just have to do some cooking and cleaning and ferrying people around. It's not hard."

Through the wall, Simon and Tracey have started a romantic chorus. "Yes! Yes! Yes! Yaaaahhhhsss!"

"Oh shut the fuck up!" I yell. "Sorry. Sorry. Not you Gem. The nymphomaniacs next door." I roll away from the wall and perch on the edge of the bed with my head in my hands. I need to put on some headphones and loud head-banging music, anything to stop me from banging my own head against my own wall.

I'm at enough of a low ebb that I just might cave in and take up Gemma's bonkers-as-batshit idea.

"The skiing's definitely not compulsory?" I ask.

"No, of course not. You'd love it here, if only you were willing to give it a go. And think about all the potential material for your writing. It's a perfect research opportunity."

"More like an opportunity to break my neck. Though I suppose at the moment that also has a certain appeal…"

"Right. That's it. You're coming even if I have to come and drag you out here myself. You're broke, you're miserable, you're practically cohabiting with your ex and that bitch next door. I'm offering you a lifeline but you're too damn stubborn or stupid to see it. Do I really need to come and get you?"

I sigh. "I don't know, Gem. I'm hardly chalet girl material."

"What, and I am?" Her laughter draws a small smile from my lips. I miss that happy sound. "At least you know how to cook, which is more than me! And look, it's nothing like you probably imagine. I mean, forget the movie." She's talking about *Chalet Girl*. We must have watched that movie about a hundred times before she left, and that was where Gemma got her soft idea to do a season of chalet-girling in the first place.

"What are the folks like?"

"Admittedly, there is the odd Burtonbridgetta and Burktonian" — That's what we call the posh kids in town — "but on the whole everyone's here to ski and have a good time. A bloody good time! Out of interest, when did you last have a good time?"

I dab my eyes with my sleeve and ignore her prod. "It's not exactly great pay though, is it?"

"It's better than no pay, you moron." Ouch. Gemma doesn't flinch from the truth. Admittedly, I've yet to find myself a job, but in a backwater market town on the edge of the Yorkshire Moors, jobs are hard to come by. Unless perhaps you're a farmer. Like Simon.

The vision of him on Boxing Day, scuffing his rain boots against the sidewalk, his ruddy cheeks ruddier than ever, flashes into my head. At the time I'd been so busy admiring him, it had taken a while for his words to sink in. He wanted a fresh start. With my next door neighbor. Who is a complete cow, by the way, so I guess she'll fit in well with the rest of his herd.

"Val, you still there?"

Stop thinking about Simon and Tracey! "Yeah." I can't help noticing it's now silent next door. Have they left the room? Or is it going to start over, my life is like the worst Groundhog Day ever imaginable.

"If you don't take this job, I might end up having to work with some brainless numbskull. You owe me! Please, Val!"

"I don't know how I'd even get there. I can't afford it."

"I can lend you the money for the fare and you can pay me back later."

"And what about Mum?"

"Oh, come on! She'll be delighted. She'll be able to turn your room into her yoga studio." This is true. My mother is a part-time nurse and part-time yoga teacher. She's also about the most positive person I know, which is pretty incredible considering she's raised me and my brother single-handedly for the last ten years. Only last night she was asking me what my plans were for the year and encouraging me to do something. Anything.

I'm silent. Chewing my lip.

"I'm not sure I'm up to talking to anyone much," I say.

"Give o'er. You never used to be such a sap. You love talking to folks. And I swear I'll look out for you. Come on. Say, yes! You'll love it here! Man, you wouldn't believe how spectacular the mountains are. You'll have plenty of spare time to read and write. You could bake to your heart's content. There's even a pool, a hot tub and a sauna, although of course, we can only use those when there aren't any guests about. You'll meet loads of interesting people. Exciting people. Hot men. You can do whatever or whoever takes your fancy!"

"That's the problem, I don't fancy anyone. I don't want to do… anything without Simon." My voice quavers. It's pathetic. I'm so disgustingly pathetic.

"Aye, maybe because you don't see anyone else, that's more likely the problem. Slime-on might sit up and take a bit of notice of you if you looked like you were having some fun. This place is teeming with fit men and you might meet someone who's not a waste of oxygen ..."

"Hmmm," I say, chewing on a fingernail. It's not the worst scheme Gemma's ever come up with. Gemma is pulling out all the stops in her persuasive arsenal, and I love her for it. "It's not the worst idea."

"Simon you bad, bad boy!" I hear Tracey yell.

That's it. I hurl my boots at the wall.

"Right then, put your money where your mouth is and put some distance between you and them. For your own sanity, if nothing else. It'll be wicked. We'll make a wicked team. And besides, I miss you."

"Awww, I miss you too." And I seem to have run out of excuses. Arguing with Gemma is like fighting a punchbag. You're never going to win.

I mumble. "Okay."

"Is that a yes?" she asks. "I have to let the owner, Leo Cloutier, know today, and you need to get your bum over here by the weekend at the latest. It's a few months, not a life sentence."

Leo Cloutier. Now there's a name for a character.

"Please, Val, be my—"

"Okay, okay, I surrender. I'll come!"

2

LEO

"I'm not investing," I say, studying the figures on my screen.

"That's disappointing, darling. I really hoped you'd see the enormous growth potential in this—"

"There *is* no growth potential. None whatsoever! Sorry, Sarah, but you're deluded. You've got as much chance of floating this as the Titanic. You're pissing your money … into a violin!" That's a French expression. She won't get it. Her French is abominable. "You're pissing into the wind!" I explain in terms more familiar to her. "If you want my advice, you'll pull out now before you lose any more money."

There is silence at the other end of the line. She'll be pouting.

"You asked for my advice and I'm simply being honest. I'm out," I add.

"Then, I'm out too, of this whole damn relationship," says Sarah.

I smile. "Right. That's fine."

"What do you mean, that's fine? Leo, I didn't—"

"Look, I've got to go. I'll call you when I get back from Méricoeur."

"Leo, you're s-such a cold b-bastard!"

I end the call because I don't want to hear her crying. *Femme idiote!* I catch Derek's eye in the driving mirror. "I'm not being sexist,"

I say defensively. "How is it someone so highly qualified and seemingly intelligent can be so stupid? She wants to jeopardize her family house and entire livelihood on some hare-brained no-chance get-rich-quick scheme and then, when she loses all her money, she'll blame it on me!"

A slight smile quirks my chauffeur's mouth, and he returns his concentration to the autoroute ahead.

Gritting my teeth, I glance at the white-washed fields and trees flying past. Why do the women I date always say they just want to have fun, but then they dig their nails in? There always seems to be an ulterior motive. Marriage. Investment. Whatever happened to pure, unadulterated, joyful sex? I suspect my capital is the only reason Sarah enticed me into her bed in the first place. I must have been crazy. She's married with kids. I mean, what sort of arsehole has an affair with a married woman with kids?

Ah yes, that'd be moi.

I clear my throat and send a quick voice message to Full Blooms asking them to arrange a delivery of sunny-colored flowers to Sarah along with my customary parting note. Okay, I'm far from perfect, but neither are happy families my thing.

Then I make my other morning calls. I check in with the partners in the Paris and London offices about the various meetings that day and offer my advice. I receive another pitch, this time one with some decent potential from an online dating app company. Despite my initial skepticism, their financial projections look sound, and I try to be open-minded, at least when it comes to business. I don't accept immediately because we need to do a bit more research, but I promise to get back to them within forty-eight hours.

"Brian, check out the online dating app Love Mine. See what you can dredge up about the company," I say, ringing one of our junior venture capitalists in London.

By the time we reach Beaune to pick up the Grand Cru I bought via telephone auction back in November, my stomach is rumbling like a freight train and all I can think about is breakfast. And, of course, Amélie, my sister. If there's a weak chink in my armor, it's Amé.

Derek pulls into the carpark of Le Jardin des Bergamotte.

"See you in an hour, Derek, okay?"

"*Oui. Dire bonjour à Amélie. Amusez-vous.*"

Amusing myself is not really the order of the day. Amé is digging in her Louboutin heels and proving as stubborn as a mule. Hugo, my older brother, refuses to interfere, but to be fair, he has a lot of strife to deal with in his own life. In my opinion, he should never have got married in the first place, and neither should Amé. This meeting with her is my last opportunity to persuade her to drop her own wedding plans.

"You know, it's never too late. If you have any doubts about Josh…"

Her chin goes up. "Doubts? Why would I have any doubts? I love him with all my heart. I cannot wait to spend the rest of my life with him and have lots of little Joshies."

Eugghh. It is enough to put me off my croissant. "You really want to live in England with a man who's in the military?"

As much as she refuses to admit it, she must be apprehensive. We spent our early childhood in England. Our father was British. It was a miserable, desperate time. I don't mind visiting, but you can't get a decent meal there and they don't know bottle of wine from a bottle of piss … and marrying a man in the soldier. By my reckoning, over the last millennium more than a quarter of that time has been spent fighting against the English. Trying to keep them out of the country. Why would she want to live with them?

"In England, in France, in Germany, in Newfoundland for all I care!" She puts on a brave smile. "I will go wherever Josh goes, and I cannot wait!"

"And if he goes to war? You'll be left kicking your heels in some miserable British army barracks. And what if he ends up… like…" I grimace and screw up my napkin.

She says nothing, but we both know I'm talking about our shit of a wife-beating English father. He's still alive, but we've disowned him. One of the few decisions Hugo, Amé and I agreed upon unanimously. When we moved to France, we put him behind us and adopted our French mother's surname. It's somewhat ironic that for years we tried to forget we had any English blood at all, and yet now Amé is talking of marrying an Englishman.

"When do you imagine you will see each other? What about the time he'll have to spend on military operations and you, with your own traveling? How well do you imagine that will work out?" I ask.

"I may give up work," she says.

"What? You love your job!" My sister is an air hostess. For as long as I can remember, she wanted to travel. Not so very surprising, I think we all wanted to fly the coop that was our family home.

"I know, but maybe I want to have my own family now and settle down."

"Oh, *mon Dieu*. No, Amé, you don't." I cannot help but laugh. "What if Josh turns out to be like Papa?"

She gasps. "Josh is nothing, *nothing*, like him! Just because he's English, you think—"

"It's not only that. You're so young. You have your whole life ahead of you and this marriage... Josh... will change everything. You're throwing your life away."

"It will all work out fine, you'll see!" says Amé, starting to get tearful.

"No, I don't see." But I do feel crap for having upset her. Her marrying Josh and a man in the military is about the worst idea she's ever had, and she's had a few. I don't mind English people, per se. I work with enough of them, but I would rather not have an English man as family. That feels a bit too close to the bone.

"If I didn't care, I wouldn't say these things. I—"

"Then don't! Don't say anything else! Go to Méricoeur and make sure Josh enjoys himself. That's all I'm asking."

The week ahead fills me with dread. Not the skiing, of course. Any excuse for skiing is fine in my book, but it means spending a week in the company of Josh Armstrong and his English Neanderthal army 'mates'. I have only met Josh twice. The second time was a mistake. I thought I might be able to persuade him to leave my sister alone, but it turns out he wasn't interested in my money. According to him, he has 'honor' and 'integrity' … Well, we'll see about that.

"Try to not to have a *pet de travers*," continues Amé. *Pet de travers* literally means to fart sideways, and it's her pet way of telling me I'm being a grumpy shit. "I want the pair of you to become friends."

"Sure." The idea of Josh and I becoming friends is about as likely as me walking on the moon.

She sips her coffee and looks thoughtful. "I'm grateful that you agreed to give the chalet up for the stag week, truly I am, and I'm even happier that you will be with Josh to keep an eye on them all."

"Only to make sure they don't destroy my place."

She puts her hand on mine and squeezes. "I know you will be civil. And make sure Josh doesn't do anything silly. He can be a little impulsive and if encouraged by his friends, I can imagine, he might feel he needs to be unnecessarily reckless …" She bites her lip, a small worry frown dimples between her brows.

Never mind his so-called friends, I'll be the first to encourage Josh … off a high mountain cliff. "I'll keep an eye on him, don't worry."

"And don't forget there's a new chalet host, Valerie. I hope she is not as attractive as Gemma. Make sure Josh … I'm sure I'm worrying about nothing, but please make sure Josh doesn't get led astray."

Now there's a capital idea. One worth sinking some money into.

"How do you think Josh would react if I turned up at the chalet, as a surprise?" she asks.

I look at her incredulously. It is a terrible idea. "Is this the reason you wanted to meet me? To ask this?"

She takes a sip of her coffee. "Is it a crazy idea? It wouldn't be for the whole time."

"*Absolutement.* Why would he possibly object?" If she turns up unexpectedly at the wrong moment, and discovers him in some sort of compromising situation … "Maybe at the end of the week. Let him have his fun with the boys first," I say, avoiding her gaze.

"I'm fun."

"Of course, you are. Call me before you come, that's all, just to check it's a convenient time."

"If you say so." She folds her napkin.

"*C'est parti!*" I say, kissing her on each cheek ten minutes later. If I have to do this stag party week, I want to get on with it. And I now feel like Machiavelli preparing to do battle with these English soldiers. In France the equivalent of a stag party is *enterrement de vie de garçon* which translates as burying the life of the boy. If I have my way, that's exactly what I'll do to Josh.

An hour later, I'm back on the road. Derek takes the exit for Geneva airport where I'm dropping him off so he can fly back home for two weeks' holiday, the lucky bastard. I have one week with this stag party and then I reckon I'll need a further week to recover. Of course, I'm not intending to stop working unless I'm actually on the piste.

While I make a few more phone calls, a plan percolates at the back of my mind involving Josh and our chalet girls... and how to garner sufficient evidence to make Amé realize she's making a terrible mistake.

It's risky, but isn't that what I spend my entire life doing — weighing up risks and deciding whether to invest my money and reputation in them? And honestly, it wouldn't be the first time I've been labeled a cold-blooded bastard.

3

VALERIE

In the first week working at *Chalet Sauveterre*, Gemma and I fall into a comfortable routine which suits us both. Generally, because she is keen to get up and get out to the slopes, she does the early shift: breakfast in the mornings, clearing plates into the dishwasher afterwards, wiping down the table and setting up for the evening. Once the guests and Gemma have cleared off and the house is quiet, like a mouse, I come out of my room and get on with the cleaning and cooking for the day. I love having the chalet to myself, imagining it's all mine.

Every day I make a cake for afternoon tea, inhaling the sweet scent of home-baking. I've also become a little addicted to Instagram, posting daily pictures of said cake, or luxurious chalet, or glorious mountains and snowy pistes (from the safety of the gondola) — if the odd hunky male happens to get caught in the frame, that's hardly my fault. In between cleaning the bathrooms and doing the housework, I keep an eye on Simon and Tracey's social media feeds too. I have to say, mine look way more interesting.

After a month, I almost feel like a local, greeted by name in the *supermarché* and *boulangerie*. When I clean, I usually put on loud music and dance my way through the chores. Afterwards I reward myself with a dip in the pool, or a sweat in the sauna, and a slice of whatever I've baked on the side for Gemma and me. And I'm writing again. I'm proud of how much I've achieved in only a few weeks: I've plotted a whole series of books and made a start on the first one. It's about a gap year student whose best laid plans go a bit haywire, but she finds romance on a vineyard. I'm happy I made the decision to come here. This is my new life. Baking. Cleaning. Writing. Checking social media...

To be honest, most days it feels like I'm on holiday. One of those active holidays where I could be learning to cook at some swanky cookery school, or doing a bootcamp for fitness addicts to shape up, or on a writing retreat. I have every intention of taking advantage of my free ski and lift pass, but apart from using it to take Instagram photos, the skiing hasn't quite happened yet despite Gemma's cajoling.

It's great working with her and a comfort to know she has my back. As agreed, Gemma does most of the 'front of house' work in the chalet because I would rather not have to engage in chitchat. Of course, I haven't stopped thinking about home and I ring Mum daily, but I've managed to stop asking about Simon. Every so often, I even hear from my smartass brother, Ben, from his ivory tower at university. It's usually to take the piss out of my Instagram. Of course, he's cottoned on that some of my photos and more inventive video footage on my social media stream captured by Gemma and her Go-pro, aren't actually honestly me. Hopefully, no-one but Mum and Ben will be any the wiser. Simon commented on a few posts lately. But, after some tough love from Gemma, I've resisted responding.

Way to go, Valerie! Like I said, I'm proud of myself.

Today though, I'm more nervous than usual. It's changeover day and although the owner is not arriving with his party of guests until tomorrow, Gemma has impressed on me that it's essential everything is perfection. Before I get on with the cleaning, I whizz up chocolate cake batter. Grabbing the key to the master suite, which is on this floor but usually kept locked, I go and open up the shutters. There's very little to do in here, just a quick polish, vacuum and dust. Momentarily I'm distracted by the incredible views, and somewhere out there Gemma is skiing her heart out along with all the other ant-sized figures. Before I leave, I'll give it a try, I tell myself.

After taking the cake out of the oven, I get started on the ground floor. The house is spread over four floors altogether. At ground level are a boot room, a drying room and garage, the swimming pool, the hot tub (outside) and sauna, a games room with a ping-pong table, and Gemma and my bedrooms with our own private terrace (if we can get out beyond the snow drift).

With regard to cleaning, the ground floor is fine; not much effort required. The next floor up, where the master suite is situated, is the most impressive with enormously high beamed ceilings in the open plan sitting room and dining area. A paved terrace wraps around the back of the house and the wall of glass windows frames another poster-perfect view of the mountains. One of my favorite spots to read and write is up on the galleried landing above where there are shelves upon shelves of books, not to mention a convenient desk and a couple of comfortable leather armchairs to curl up on. On this floor, although the television room needs a quick vacuum, the mess is again minimal.

Propping the door to the terrace open, I go outside to fetch fresh firewood, stacking it in the metal circular frame beside the grand stone fireplace ready for the next day. Taking advantage of the sound system, I put on some workout music and head upstairs to the second floor where there are four bedrooms, all with en suites. So far, so good, but it's on this top floor that the day develops into what I imagine would feel like unexpectedly teetering on the edge of a black ski run.

After, rapidly stripping down the beds in the first three bedrooms, throwing all the used linen into a laundry hatch which goes straight to the basement, I open the door to the fourth bedroom and — Hell's bells! — I'm hit by an unholy stench. Mother of all archangels, what is that? Where is it coming from?

Warily, I head toward the bathroom. There are towels strewn on the floor, a large yellow piss puddle on the tiles, and, not only that, if I'm not mistaken, a used condom discarded in the corner.

"Ewww! Disgusting! What sort of animal…" Clamping a hand across my face, I peer in further. To top off all this loveliness, the toilet bowl looks like an elephant has taken a dump in there.

"What the hell?" Where do I even start?

Trying to hold my nose with one hand and the mop with another, I begin to wipe the floor. It's no good: I need both hands to hold the mop handle. Holding my breath, as quickly as I can, I mop the floor, dunk in the bucket, and mop again. Really, I could do with goggles, or some sort of protective face gear.

"Of all the bloody filthy, dirty pigs … Someone has shit a brick shed!" Grimacing, I mop a pathway toward the toilet, and press the flush. The contents of the toilet bowl begin to rise.

Oh no! "No, no, no, no, no! Do not overflow! Don't you bloody dare!" I step back in a hurry, slip on the wet floor and kick the bucket behind me, which hurtles toward the wall. The contents slosh up the tiles, the bucket tips and crashes over emptying its contents all over the tiles … and me. "You have got to be fucking kidding!" I shriek.

My jeans and socks are soaked in a stinking foul combination of soapy water, muck from the floor and urine! *"Ewwww!"* I howl. Even my t-shirt is splashed. And meanwhile, the contents of the toilet bowl are still on the rise.

I'm not really the praying sort, but I start jabbering, "Please God! Mother of God! Any gods at all up there! Please make it stop!" There's a sucking sound like a bog monster gargling and … and … the tide subsides. "Oh, thank you, thank you, thank you!"

I look around me in despair, not sure quite where to begin. Putting the bucket in the oval bath, I start refilling it with water. While that's happening, I peel off my sodden socks and my splashed t-shirt and jeans, and throw them in the bathtub. I'm tempted to get in and have a good soak myself, but there's a lingering odor in this room and I'm already traumatized enough to want to get the hell out of here as fast as I can. "Bloody hell!" I mutter, wiping my brow with the back of my wrist as I turn off the tap.

I hear footsteps on the stairs.

"Gemma!" I yell. "Get your backside in here! You never said anything about being exposed to toxic waste in your job description. I should be paid double for this. Men who piss all over the floor and shit like dinosaurs and can't manage to chuck their condoms in a bin need castrating, or worse!"

Growling, I pick up the condom in my pink gloved hands. Dangling it between gloved finger and thumb, I go to the bathroom door to show her the offending item ... and shriek. There is a man in a suit standing in the bedroom doorway.

"Holy crap and bloody Nora! Who the hell are you?"

"Clearly not Nora." Raising one eyebrow, in a very casual manner, he looks me over.

"Get out!" I drop the condom on the bathroom floor and try to cover myself, grateful I still have my bra and knickers on! "Get out immediately! What do you think you're doing, walking in here uninvited? This is private property. Get out before I call the police!" I grab the mop and brandish it at him.

"*Eughh*! Be careful with that! You would not want it dripping on my carpet."

He's right. He's also French. And did he say, *my* carpet?

I plonk the mop back in the bucket and hastily chuck the condom in the dustbin while I'm at it. Shaking, I peer back into the bedroom, but he's gone. What the hell should I do now? I'm not going to put my soiled clothes back on. And who the hell was he? An intruder? An axe murderer?

I tiptoe out onto the landing. And then creep down the stairs in my undies and rubber gloves. I know why imagination sometime gets the better of me, but God, I could have been assaulted. He may have done nothing but scare the bloody living daylights out of me, but still, I need to make absolutely sure he's gone.

He hasn't.

From the stairwell, I can see straight into the kitchen. He's in there doing God only knows what. Finding a knife? Oh holy shit, and I can't even call the police because the kitchen is where I've left my handbag and phone. How would I describe him anyway? I've no clue what the French words are for tall, dark and bloody hair-raising ...

I grab a fur throw from one of the couches and wrap it around myself as best I can. I stand at the bottom of the stairs wondering what I should do next, run for it or see what he's up to? I can hear him in the kitchen humming a tune. With my heart in my mouth, I take a few cautious steps back up toward the first floor, pausing again to listen. What's he doing in there? Is that coffee I can smell? Yes, the cheeky bastard is only making himself a coffee.

"Would you like a coffee?" he shouts unexpectedly, making me jump.

Is he talking to me? Or is there another intruder in here somewhere?

He sticks his head out of the kitchen door and raises his eyebrows. "I dig the cave woman look. How do you take it?"

I very nearly fall backwards down the stairs. How do I take what?

"Excuse me, what do you think you're doing?" My voice sounds very proper and English (my best Burtonbridgetta) — but also shaky. "Please leave immediately. This is private property!"

"Yes, I know that," he says, disappearing again. "You're baking smells good!" he shouts. "May I help myself to a slice?"

My heart is still hammering, but if he meant me any harm would he be offering me coffee and complimenting my cooking skills?

"Certainly not," I say from the kitchen doorway, still in two minds about whether to make a run for it. Instead, I snatch my handbag from the counter. Clutching it against my chest, I grope for my phone. "Who are you? What do you want?"

His hand hovers over my cake. "Apart from this cake? I—"

"Get your hands off my cake! You can't come in here and help yourself to stuff. *Arretez* or else!"

He puts his hands beside his head in mock surrender and throws me a lopsided smile. I'll make his face even more lopsided if he doesn't leave!

"Or else, what is it you shall do, *mon petit diable?*"

I've no idea what he's just said, but his arrogance and bloody amusement are infuriating. "Or I'm calling the police!" I shout, delighted my fingers have finally located my phone. I dial 999.

"I wouldn't do that."

"Wouldn't you? Well, I would." I grab the knife that he's laid on the kitchen counter. "Don't move a muscle. Stay right where you are!" I point the knife at him and put my phone to my ear.

"You dialed the wrong number. It's seventeen for police," he informs me.

I gawp. "Seventeen? What do you mean?"

"In France you dial one seven if you want police. Eighteen for fire service. Fifteen for ambulance. If in doubt, stick with one hundred and twelve for general emergencies. You should know that, if you're working here. I presume you *are* meant to be working."

My cheeks flash with heat, and his smile widens.

"But as I said, I wouldn't bother. Calling the police." He turns his back on me again. There is something about his tone that is horribly deflating. And he seems to know his way around the kitchen rather well, making himself at home.

Calm yourself. I take a deep breath. "Okay. Enough fun and games. Who are you?"

He looks over his shoulder and smiles again. A smile that could start an avalanche.

My heart skips a beat.

"Clearly no-one of any importance. A French burglar." He laughs, amused by his own bloody joke. He busies himself getting mugs out of the overhead cupboard and pouring coffee; I'm busy trying to figure out if he's actually someone from the agency, or one of the guests due tomorrow who's shown up prematurely, or a friend of Gemma's. Or just a very cocky, incredibly arrogant French criminal.

"Are you a friend of Gemma's?"

"Non. I am not a *friend* of Gemma... We have a different kind of relationship."

Oh, one of them! A lover I don't know about.

He leans against the counter inspecting me. His dark brown eyes should be red, like surgical lasers, but they're molten brown, like liquid chocolate.

"So you didn't tell me, how do you like it?" he asks.

A nervous laugh escapes me, and I fold my arms across my chest. "You should be the one answering *my* questions, not the other way around!"

"Ah, oui. I should mind my own onions."

"Sorry?" Hold on, I'm apologizing now?

"*S'occuper de ses onions*, we say here in France. It means mind your own business. So you really don't want coffee at all?" His voice is a horrible distraction too. I don't want to admit it's sexy — aren't all French accents? — but there's no denying it: a honeyed-tone which in different circumstances could be a warm, lingering caress.

"Did the agency send you?" My voice on the other hand is shrill, and shaky, and being broad Yorkshire about as sexy as a Yorkshire pudding with gravy.

He compresses his mouth in a hard line — I think he could be trying to stop himself from laughing again — and shakes his head.

"If you're a guest, I should inform you the arrival date isn't until tomorrow." I thought the guests were mostly English though, apart from...oh sweet Lord...the owner.

I close my eyes and pray. "You're not Monsieur Cloutier, are you?" *Please say you're not. Please say I'm wrong.*

"An interesting pronunciation, mademoiselle, but yes, Monsieur Leo Cloutier at your service." He bows like a courtier from days gone by.

I put a hand against the doorframe to steady myself. The owner. Why the hell didn't I think of that sooner? Why didn't he tell me? Terrific. I might as well hand in my notice and leave now.

"Why didn't you say?" I falsetto laugh.

"*Bof.*" He shrugs. "I was going to, but you interrupted, and I have to be honest, it was all rather entertaining."

"Do you have any ID?"

He gives me a look. "Seriously?"

"Seriously. You could be anyone. I'd rather be sure..."

Sighing, he pulls out his wallet and removes a card. I snatch it from his hand.

It's a black American Express card with the initials L .M. Cloutier across the bottom. It's not exactly photo ID ...

"Would you like to go through the rest of the contents of my wallet?"

I swallow and put his bank card on the counter next to him. "No, that's fine. I'm very sorry. Welcome to ... your own chalet," I finish lamely.

"You sure I can't tempt you with a coffee?" he asks again.

"Oh, I suppose... yes, actually, I think maybe I will. Thank you very much. With a splash of milk, please." And maybe a slosh of whiskey to lend me some courage. Behind his back, I put a fist to my forehead. Dumb, dumb, dumb.

"Ah yes, weak and milky and no doubt frothy," he says, which is a character assassination if ever I heard one. There is nothing wrong with liking a splash of milk in your coffee. Of course, he takes his black and strong.

I put on my bravest smile.

A wry smile flickers on his lips as he hands me my mug. "So tell me, Valerie, do you usually clean my chalet in only your underwear?"

I splutter over my coffee and put it down. He knows my name and the way he says it has raised goosebumps on my arms. "I had a mishap with the mop and bucket."

"Of course, you did."

"I thought the toilet was going to overflow because it was blocked, or something, and I tripped over the bucket and knocked it over." How to impress my new employer. "I'm not usually clumsy, I swear."

He nods his head looking serious, or possibly bored. It's hard to say. He sips his coffee, takes his phone out of his pocket, and has a conversation with someone in rapid French. As if I'm now the bloody intruder. Actually, he really could be calling the police for all I know. Unfortunately, my schoolgirl French is ill-equipped to translate. Ending the call, he says, "Sorted," and walks out.

I trail behind. "What's sorted?"

"A plumber will come here this afternoon to check everything is in working order. You'll be here, of course, preferably in a few more clothes."

You'll be here. That sounds rather like an order. And he looks like he's used to giving orders. But maybe this means I still have a job. "Okay."

"Where is Gemma? Should she not be helping you?" he asks.

Oh shit. She's entitled to time off, but I don't want him to think she's shirking and judging from the tone of his voice he's no longer amused (if he ever was). "She's... um... running an errand," I lie, not wanting to get her into trouble as well. I avoid looking at him.

When the silence stretches, I'm forced to look up. His eyes have narrowed and his upper lip is curled like I smell bad, which is not beyond the realm of possibility considering the mess I've been dealing with and how much of an emotional lather I'm currently in.

"Really." The extra roll he gives to his r makes my stomach swoop in terror as does his expression which is decidedly sour.

"Yes, really," I manage to squeak.

4

LEO

When Gemma gets back, we have a little chat. I want to get rid of Valerie. I explain my predicament: I am not happy she is cleaning in her underwear. It is very unprofessional. Imagine if one of the guests found her like that. I do not want to imagine what may or may not happen.

In fact, my imagination has been playing all sorts of bizarre tricks on me ever since I first laid eyes on Valerie, but Gemma doesn't need to know that I was fantasizing about screwing her on the kitchen counter. And in the shower. Maybe the shower first to make sure she wasn't contaminated. But she has definitely been messing with my mind and that is unacceptable.

"We need her, Leo. She's a great cook and if you want to make a good impression with your stag party friends, you have to keep her. And besides, she's my best friend. If she goes ... I go."

I sigh. *Fucking women! Merde!* They are all so exasperating. "Who said anything about wanting to make a good impression," I say through gritted teeth. Amé's pleading face drifts into my head. "*Bof*! Very well. I give her one more week. A trial. But any more nonsense, even the slightest slip and she's finished. Get her in here. I need to talk to you both."

Gemma goes out grinning and comes back chuckling with a slightly more remorseful Valerie in tow.

"So tomorrow, my guests will be arriving for this ..." — the very idea of it brings a sour taste to my mouth— "bachelor stag party affair." I curse Amé for making me have to deal with this whole miserable event. "I hope it will not prove too difficult for you. Please make sure you are dressed appropriately at all times." I don't look at Valerie, but it should be clear who I'm addressing. "Anyway, the following week, I shall be staying on here by myself, alone, so it should be quieter. You will be able to relax a little to compensate for what may be a tough week of... whatever it is Englishmen do at these *stag* parties. If there are any problems whatsoever, if any of them overstep the boundaries of what is respectable behavior, if anything happens, I want to know about it. Do you understand?"

Gemma and Valerie nod, but say nothing. However, they are clearly amused, Gemma grinning like a loon and Valerie biting her lip.

"Would you care to share the joke?" I snap.

"No joke. I'm still just thinking about Val in her cleaning outfit when you arrived..." She sniggers. "Never mind me. So what entertainment do you have planned for the lads?" Her eyes flick mischievously toward Valerie again.

"We shall be skiing and maybe some drinking, what else do you suggest?" I ask.

"Ah, well, I'm no expert, I've only ever been on a hen party, but I think it's customary for the lads to, you know, play silly pranks on each other, do some drinking games, dress up, that sort of thing..." Gemma raises her eyebrows.

I wish she would stop grinning. I am not finding this amusing at all.

"Perhaps that is what Josh, the groom, was referring to when he texted me." Grabbing my phone, I scroll through the many messages which have come in today, trying to find his. I think I may have deleted it already. "*Putain*! I honestly have no idea what he expects! Do you have any ideas?"

Gemma gives me a few hair-raising suggestions.

Merde. "You will have to assist me! What I would like—"

The distant sound of the oven bleeping in the kitchen interrupts me. I glare at Valerie.

"Excuse me," says Valerie, "I'd better go and rescue that." Her pert little rump scuttles out the door. It is just as well. There is something about Valerie's pert little rump which makes me think of spanking ...

As I discuss plans for the week with Gemma, my train of thought keeps getting derailed by the image of Valerie. Over my knee. Or on the bed, rump in the air. *Merde!* She definitely needs to go. As soon as this week is over.

5

VALERIE

The slamming of car doors heralds the arrival of Gemma and Leo back from the airport with the stag party. Oh, joy of joys. My stomach churns as I hear all the male voices downstairs.

So far, my working experience in the chalet has been pleasant (with the possible exception of meeting Leo and the bog monster episode). Mainly it's entailed catering for families or groups of skiing friends, but now we have the French owner breathing like a dragon down our necks along with a rowdy group of men. I cannot imagine it will be easy. I cannot help feeling like the honeymoon period working in this chalet is well and truly over. But who knows, perhaps it'll provide some more ideas for my writing, and I suppose I should be grateful I still have a job. I think it was a close shave.

This morning Leo looked irritated to see me still here, after which he clearly avoided even acknowledging my presence — miserable git. Gemma reassured me last night, after she'd spoken to him in his office, that out of the kindness of his black heart Leo has agreed to let me stay on trial for another week, and that everything will be fine, if I can just keep my head down and keep my distance from him—which suits me. I know I'm making a sweeping generalization, so forgive me, but I have found it to be true that the French can be a little moody at the best of times. I don't think they care for us Brits. Well, if you can imagine the very worst of the French, that's Leo today. I bet he's going to be a bundle of laughs on his stupid stag party.

The mind boggles at how he could possibly be friends with them. Of course, it's bloody obvious why Leo has agreed to let me to stay on for a week. Who else is going to clean up all their shit? He needs me.

That makes me feel just a little bit smug. And I'm intrigued to see how Leo and this bunch of English squaddies rub along.

I can hear Gemma explaining loudly about the boot room, the sauna, the swimming pool, the games room, the cinema and all the downstairs facilities. She wouldn't make a bad sergeant-major herself. She's even got Leo marching to her tune.

The stag party and the grumpy French bastard troop up the stairs. I keep out of sight and let my ears do all the work. Interestingly, they don't sound like the sort of soldiers I've met from Catterick before. This lot sound posh. Maybe they're officers. How the hecky thump did Leo come to be best man to one of them?

While Gemma divvies everyone off into their rooms, I focus on cooking bacon and preparing all the Bloody Mary ingredients as instructed, pretty much hiding out in the kitchen until Gemma pokes her head through the door.

"Val, don't be shy. Come and meet everyone," she says, winking and picking up the jug of Bloody Mary and tray of glasses. "Bring out your bacon butties."

Grabbing the plate of bacon, lettuce and tomato rolls, I follow her out.

"This is Val, gents," says Gemma, "the other chalet host. She hasn't been here quite as long as me. As you'll maybe tell from our accents, we're both from the best part of England, Yorkshire."

"God's own country," says one.

"Eee by gum," says another. Great, they're taking the piss already.

As Gemma starts giving them the spiel, avoiding eye contact, I pass around the plate of BLT rolls.

The first man I get to takes his time, his hand hovering over the plate. I look up; he's looking directly down my cleavage. "Perfect baps," he says, smiling, and I accidentally upend the plate into his lap.

"Shit! I'm so sorry!" My arms flap because I'm not sure whether to retrieve the bacon and bread rolls and lettuce and tomatoes now decorating his crotch, or if that would be deemed inappropriate and I'm just waiting for Leo to rip into me. I look around, but he's not there.

Thankfully Gemma, laughing her bloody head off, comes to my rescue.

"Special treatment for the groom, eh," she jokes, completely unfazed.

That's the groom?

Gemma scoops up the disassembled bacon 'baps' from his lap. "Must be your lucky day, Josh. Baps in the lap, ey?"

"I'd rather a lap dance," he says, licking his lips and grinning at Gemma. She smiles warmly, but I'm mortified and totally tongue-tied.

As soon as I can, I rush out, almost bumping into Leo on his way into the sitting room. He has an unpleasant smile plastered on his face. I wonder if he knows I messed up already. No doubt he'll cite it as another reason to sack me at the end of the week.

From the relative safety of the kitchen, through the serving hatch, I continue to listen to Gemma.

"So the pair of us'll be looking after you, but Val is still learning, so go easy on her lads, right? "

"I'll go easy on her," says some smart Alec.

"I know she's dead pretty, but don't get any ideas, or you'll have me to deal with," says Gemma, a steely tone in her voice. There is more muffled laughter.

I press my hands to my flaming cheeks. I feel about as pretty as a baboon's butt. How am I going to cope with a week of this?

"If you've any questions about the area, I'm the one to ask," continues Gemma.

"Or possibly me," says Leo. There's no mistaking that French accent.

"Of course, sorry, I was forgetting for a moment you were here, boss. We've got a great week of skiing ahead, if the weather holds. The forecast is a bit mixed, but there's plenty of fun to be had in town if the weather turns and you can always chill out in the pool or sauna, play a bit of ping-pong et cetera. First thing to do right now though is to get all your ski kit sorted. Ten minutes long enough to get ourselves ready to go?"

There are calls to the affirmative. These lads are like putty in Gemma's very capable hands.

"Meet you back here in ten, then. No time to lose. The snow is waiting."

Gemma comes into the kitchen and gives me a hug. "Easy as pie. Alright duck?"

"Apart from dying of embarrassment, I'll be fine."

"You will be. They're harmless. Once you get to know them, you'll think they're champion."

Champion tossers, maybe.

I remove the chocolate and raspberry muffins from the oven and inhale. *Keep calm and carry on baking. It's only a week.*

This job would be wonderful without any clients.

Unfortunately, several hours later, they're back again.

I hear the men singing and shouting long before the front door blasts open. "Boots off!" shouts Gemma.

The sound of skis being racked is followed by feet stomping up the stairs.

Gemma pops her head around the door. "Sorry we've been a while. We got sidetracked at the Roley. You been okay, stuck here? Smells delicious! I'm starving." Her face looks flushed, perhaps by the cold weather or possibly from alcohol. "They lads are going for a dip in the pool before supper. I'll have a quick shower and then come and give you a hand. God, those muffins look good!"

I hand her the tray. "Can you hand them around before you shower? I just have to … um … tidy up a bit in here."

"Coward," she says, pocketing one as she heads out with the tray.

Through the serving hatch, I can hear the men making appreciative noises. That's good enough and close enough for me.

An hour later, Gemma helps me finish off preparing the evening meal while the sound of muffled shouting filters up from the depths of the house. Once all the vegetables are peeled and prepped, Gemma nudges me. "Come on, let's take a squiz!"

"They might see us!" I hiss as she trots off toward the stairs, beckoning me.

"Nonsense, they're far too busy drowning each other!" Standing at one side of the swimming pool entrance, she leans sideways to take a sneaky peek through the glass. And snorts with laughter. "Oh my God, you have to check this out. Instagram gold!" Not quite so surreptitiously, she takes her phone out of her pocket, stretches her arm in front of the glass door and snaps a couple of photos.

Of course, like a fool, I follow. She steps aside to let me get a better view. The men are prancing about in fluorescent mankinis. *Mankinis!* They look flaming ridiculous.

"Take a shot for Simon!" Gemma suggests.

I snap a couple of shots with the camera on my phone.

Behind me, someone clears their throat. Someone rather manly. I whip around to find Leo standing at the bottom of the stairs with a towel draped around his midriff and no mankini in sight.

"What are you two doing?"

Gemma almost falls over herself laughing as she barges past him and runs back up the stairs.

"Sorry, we were ... I was ... just going ... this way ... to my room." I avoid his eyes, but his muscled chest and stomach have me tripping over my feet. As I stumble past, I force myself to look up and his eyes bore holes in me.

"If you're going to your room, why are you heading upstairs?"

I cringe. "I changed my mind?"

"*Va te faire cuire un oeuf,*" he says.

I have no idea what he means — something about cooking and an egg? — but the irritated tone is easy enough to translate.

Later that evening, once I've regained my cool and we've served up the last course of the meal, we hear the sound of ringing glass.

"You giving a speech, Leopold?" asks one of the men.

There are a few guffaws.

"So, I have never had the pleasure of being included in a stag party previously," says Leo, sounding a lot French, a lot pompous, and not a lot like it's a genuine pleasure. "Joshua, I am — How shall I put it? — honored to be your best man. But I am grateful for the ideas and suggestions from your friends for the week ahead. This afternoon has already been a revelation."

I bet it has.

"Because all of this is new to me," — he pauses again — "Benoit and Antoine have kindly offered to take charge of the activities for the week, with my aid if necessary. Unfortunately, I have rather a lot of work to do, which may prevent me from joining you with everything."

There we go, making excuses already.

"—and so without further ado, I shall hand over to Benoit."

There are a few more ripe comments.

"Why the French names?" I whisper to Gemma.

"Leo's team has been given French names. Anyone who forgets has to do a forfeit. Will, the other lad in Leo's team, is Guillaume." Gemma grins like it's a great jest.

6

LEO

Leo

It is fucking horrible. A woeful humiliating affair. Traipsing around Méricoeur after dinner with a staggering bunch of chinless English half-wits. I try to make my excuses to leave, only to be informed by Benoit that our team will be penalized five points if I 'cop out'. This is another new rule. These English bastards move the goalposts every five minutes. I do not trust my team mates any more than the other team, however, I am not a good loser. I know this. My brother, Hugo, when he forces me to play pétanque (French bowls) reminds me of this every time I lose. It's bad enough losing against my brother, but the thought of losing against Josh is totally unbearable. Unfortunately, to win means out-drinking and out-performing these morons.

It wouldn't be quite so painful if I didn't keep bumping into people I know in Méricoeur. They want to know why I'm hanging out with a bunch of English and then, naturally, I'm obliged to explain one of them is my future brother-in-law. There is the look of surprise, followed by the look of distaste, followed by the pitying look of rather-you-than-me-you-unfortunate-bastard. To which I concur. And drink to drown my sorrows. There is no end of drinking tonight.

We arrive en masse the worse for wear at La Belle Hélène, and I spot Gemma and Valerie deep in conversation in one of the booths. I'm going to leave them be, but someone calls my name. *Ah merde.* It's Gaspard, the most lecherous goat in Méricoeur, and he's sitting in the same booth as them.

I leave the guys at the bar and make my way over.

"Leo, I heard you were in town. How long are you staying here for?" asks Gaspard, playing up his French accent and looking shiftier than a Catholic avoiding confession. I wonder what bullshit he's been spouting to Gemma and Valerie.

"Do you mean in Méricoeur or this bar?"

"Mericoeur," says Gaspard with a wheezing laugh. "I know many of the ladies will be delighted to know you're back."

"I very much doubt that." I'm swaying a little, so I sit down beside Gemma. Gaspard has pretty much got Valerie penned into the corner. "What is going on?" I stare hard at Gaspard.

"Gaspard is giving us some skiing tips," says Gemma, focused on flipping a bar mat and catching it before it lands.

"I bet he is," I say.

"Valerie would like to take a skiing lesson with me," explains Gaspard with a greasy smile.

I look at Valerie, and she looks at her drink. "That's not quite true," she says.

I'm not sure why the idea of Gaspard teaching her anything irritates the hell out of me, other than I'm possibly drunk and feeling somewhat protective of my employees, even Valerie and her skimpy knickers and lovely breasts, which I will not think about. Not at all. I keep my eyes fixed on Gaspard. "If she doesn't want a skiing lesson, don't hassle her," I say, my lips feeling a little numb.

"It's not that I don't *want* to ski," says Valerie, her eyes blinking like an owl's in the dim bar light. "I'd like to learn. I mean, I should make the most of my time here, shouldn't I?" She shakes her head and smiles warmly at Gaspard. "I'm just not sure I'm ready yet."

"I can make you ready," says Gaspard, practically rubbing his hands with glee.

I want to puke. I better not puke. Gaspard must be twice her age, and he has his arm slung along the top of the seat behind her.

"*Bof*, I can give you a lesson for free," I say, surprising myself as much as anyone else. "There's no need to bother yourself, Gasp—"

"It's no problem. I'd be delighted to teach Valerie. I'm sure I can fit you in at lunchtime tomorrow," he says, leering at her cleavage, and if my eyes aren't fooling me, twiddling with her fucking hair.

"*Non*! We wouldn't want you going hungry and missing your lunch, Gaspard. This is my responsibility, after all. Valerie is my employee, and, with me, it'll cost her nothing. I was a ski instructor in Méricoeur not so very many years ago," I explain to her. She doesn't look very reassured or impressed. "I'm sure I haven't forgotten all the *tricks*," I say, switching my gaze back to Gaspard. He winces and drinks his beer.

"Oh, thank you, but there's no need to go out of your way. I know how busy you are," says Valerie.

I turn my eyes back to her. It is like watching tennis. I feel dizzy already. "I shall make time." Her eyes blink again. It's a little hypnotic.

"Oh, but, as my employer, I'm sure—"

"Exactly. I'm your employer and you should take my advice."

She closes her mouth, tucks a strand of hair behind her ear and says nothing. Beside me, Gemma cracks up laughing.

I twist around to look at her. "What?"

She stops and bites her lip. "Nothing. I'm sure I could give you a lesson for that matter too, Val," says Gemma. "It's not exactly rocket science."

"Exactly. We shall take care of Valerie. No need to bother yourself any longer Gaspard. You may go."

"And what if I don't want to go?" He sits up.

I glare. I would like to wrench him out of the booth and throw him across the room.

"Oy, Leopold, you French frog!" someone shouts from the bar. "Boat race."

"I think you're needed at the bar," says Valerie, perhaps sensing trouble.

I tear my eyes from Gaspard.

"Oooh, I'm ace at boat races," says Gemma. "Come on, let's go join in!" She pushes me up and out of the seat.

"Valerie, join us," I say, and make a point of waiting until Gaspard has let her out. She edges past me, leaving a tantalising whiff of spring flowers and disappointment.

"Leave those English girls alone. I do not want to have to clear up the fucking mess you leave behind," I snarl at Gaspard.

※

The first person I see the next morning is Valerie. She looks bright-eyed, bubbly and so fresh-faced it makes my fists curl and my head throb.

"Good morning, Leo!" She places a basket of freshly baked bread and croissants on the table.

I grunt, and she retreats to the kitchen.

Why the hell did I drink so much last night? What sort of torturous mess has Amé ensnared me in. A week from hell. We didn't get back until four in the morning and half the day has already gone. I want to get out on the slopes and inhale some clean air and make the most of what's left of a day's skiing, preferably before any of those other idiots wake up and drag me into more so-called fun and games.

"Would you like a coffee?" asks Valerie through the hatch.

"Yes."

"About the skiing lesson …" she says tentatively.

"What skiing lesson?" I put my head in my hands. The memory of bumping into her and Gemma and bloody Gaspard resurface. I vaguely remember insisting on giving her a ski lesson, but if she thinks I'm going to be held to that she can think again.

"Please don't feel—"

"About my offer—"

She looks through the service hatch.

"You were saying?" I attempt to hold my irritation in check. No way, I'm offering to take her skiing.

"I was just going to say, please don't feel obliged. I think you'd probably had rather a lot of alcohol last night, and I don't want you to think I'd take advantage of that."

A bark of laughter escapes me and I have to put my head in my hands again. As if *she* could take advantage of *me*. I'd like to see her try. No, I wouldn't. I most definitely would not like Valerie to try to take advantage of me. Gingerly, I raise my head again.

"So," she says, a pink tongue flickering between her lips. "No bother. I'm sure if I want a lesson, Gaspard would happily—"

"*Non*. Let's bother." Maybe I'll have to have more words with Gaspard. It's not that long since he tried to take advantage of Amé and she's as proficient a skier as you'd ever see on the piste. Thank God, I'd found out about that little episode before the situation got out of hand. "When I say I'm going to do something, I do it."

"What, even if you don't want to?" she asks, smirking slightly.

"I recall you said you wanted to make the most of being here. Today the conditions for skiing look perfect." And more the fucking shame that I'll be on the nursery slopes.

Her mouth compresses into a pout. "Okay then. If you insist. That'd be ... um ... delightful."

Delightful? She could not sound less sincere if she tried.

"Right. I have some business to deal with first," and I need to find some painkillers, "and then we'll go."

"Fine."

I'd love to know what is going through that mind of hers. She tucks a strand of dark hair behind her ear again; the same nervous gesture as I'd noticed the night before. Perhaps I'm making her nervous. I attempt a smile, but it feels more like a grimace.

She disappears behind the serving hatch before I can say anything else.

An hour later, with still no sign of the others, I find Valerie in her apron, bending over the oven. I have to say this for her, as well as a pretty face, she has a derriere that drives me insane. But then I already knew that. She turns around with a cake tin in her gloved hands and a smile on her face, spots me and nearly drops it.

"Are you planning on feeding an army?" I ask. There is already a pile of savory scones sitting on the side.

Her eyes whip up to meet mine and she sets the cake tin on the workbench with a clatter. "Yes, I guess. They are soldiers, after all. I imagine they'll have ferocious appetites because of their hangovers."

Not nearly as ferocious as my temper.

"My brother always says—"

"When are you planning on getting ready for our ski lesson?" I demand.

"Oh, yes, that. I didn't think you were really serious. If you'd rather not—"

"Do I look serious?" She says nothing. "I'd rather you went and got changed. All this," I wave my hand at her baking, "can wait."

"I suppose."

"*Bien*. And wake up Gemma. She should have been up fucking hours ago. Drinking with the guys is no excuse to miss work. I'll see you in the boot room in five minutes."

I leave her wiping her hands on her apron, looking flustered.

7

VALERIE

Valerie

Leo is one heck of a grumpy git. His sour face gets even uglier once he learns I haven't yet got any ski kit. He marches me to another chalet where he has words with an elderly man. Skis and poles and ski boots are brought out. I've no idea what they talk about, but the man is doing lots of nodding and pulling his whiskers, his eyes twinkling merrily at me as if he knows something I don't. And then Leo marches me to the nursery slopes.

I have to be honest. I'm expecting him to shout at me, but Leo is surprisingly quiet and patient, even though I'm the most ungainly, uncoordinated, unenthusiastic person to ever disgrace the slope.

He explains how to negotiate the magic carpet up the hill; I explain that he really doesn't have to tell me every *leetle* thing because if toddlers are managing to travel uphill without falling off, so can I.

He demonstrates how to side-step up the snowy incline and get myself into position ready to ski; I demonstrate how to get my skis tangled and trip over my own two feet.

He unravels me and sets me back upright. Then he shows me the simple principles of how to turn and snow-plough; I show him how to fail at turning, how to parallel ski at high speed down the slope, and how to wipe out — thankfully missing the line of kids laughing their little behinds off at me.

Leo glides to a graceful stop and pulls me back to my feet again, holding me steady so I don't career off down the mountain before he gives the word. I can't see his eyes because they're hidden behind his ski glasses, but I can see his lips twitching. Right, perhaps this is how he gets his kicks — seeing me make a prize tit of myself. Again.

"Enough now, Leo. Thank you for your very kind instruction. I want to practice by myself. I really think it's high time you should go and do some proper skiing."

His chin turns fractionally toward the mountain peaks. Enough for me to admire his square stubbled jawline and think what a shame it's wasted on someone so ... so ... unromantic. In every other regard, that is, in terms of his chiseled looks, he would make a fine male protagonist.

"I am enjoying myself," he says.

"Liar."

A smile fleets across his lips and the lines either side of his mouth dimple. "It's true. It's a stunning day, is it not? And I have taken some wonderful photos," he says.

You bet his butt he has — of me in a heap in the snow.

"And, I have to confess," he continues, "I have not laughed this much in a long while."

Laughing at me, not with me. I dig my ski poles into the ground and inhale deeply. *Calm yourself, Val.* "I'm pleased you find me so entertaining."

He smiles ruefully. "Is that such a bad thing?"

I don't answer. I bang some of the snow off my skis with my ski poles, trying to pretend I know what the hell that is all about.

"How about, I leave you for one hour, and then I return to see if you have mastered the baby slope? I think you will be safe here." His eyebrows rise above his glasses.

"Is that a challenge?"

His smile broadens, and my stomach does a frightened little flip.

"If you like. Let's see if when I return you can make it the whole way down the piste without falling over at my feet. If you can, then I shall consider my job done. If you cannot, then I shall have to give you another lesson tomorrow. *D'accord?*"

No, I don't *d'accord*! What I'd like is the opportunity to bunk off. But something about the set of his shoulders and mouth, and the fact I don't want Leo to think he's employed a total wimp, makes me grit my teeth. Besides, there are kids half my height whizzing down the slope with no problem. How hard can it be? "I accept your challenge, but rest assured, I will not fall at your feet, physically or metaphorically."

He grins. "As you might say, the proof will be in the pudding, *mon petit diable*. When I return, I expect to see you gliding down this slope like a swan, not in a tangle like an ugly duckling. *Á bientot.*"

Me, an ugly duckling? The arrogant bastard touches his hat as if saluting me and skis off like he's about to do a pirouette. *Bloody swan, of course I'm a bloody swan*, I tell myself. I will not even think ugly thoughts.

Damn. Why didn't I just bail when I had the opportunity? My pride has a lot to answer for. My pride, not unlike a certain Frenchman I know, deserves a kick in the nuts.

I force myself to keep practicing, already dreading the fact I'm going to have to put on a 'performance' for Leo in an hour. But by the time he returns, I have completed five runs down the nursery slopes without any mishaps.

"Easy peasy," I tell him, sounding more confident than I feel.

"Let us hope so," he mutters, "for both our sakes."

I do everything perfectly. I get into position and set my sights on the bottom of the slope. I take it slow and steady. I might not look like much of a swan with my backside stuck out, but so long as I don't actually fall over, I won't have to suffer Leo and his smirk for much longer.

In snow-plough, I traverse the slope. I grind to a halt and realize perhaps I am being a little overcautious. I turn downhill and pick up momentum. I traverse again. A couple of shouting kids whistle by, nearly unhinging me, but I continue. Picking up confidence, I traverse a third time, a little braver and a little quicker now.

Out of the corner of my eye, I see Leo glide past. He has his phone out and is taking photos of me. The bastard. I wobble and nearly come a cropper. He waits at the bottom, taking more snaps. I try my best to look like a seasoned professional and point my skis directly toward him. My speed picks up. Looking up, I see he's not actually taking photos any more, but talking to someone on his phone and not even watching. I might plough into him if he doesn't move, and soon. I try to persuade my skis to move left, but there's a bunch of kids there. I try for the right, but it's as if I'm now stuck in tramlines headed for Leo. He'll look up and see me. He'll—

"Leo!"

Leo has enough time to put his arms out before I pile into him. We end up in a tangle on the floor, me lying on top of him. It takes a moment for us both to catch our breaths. "What are you doing? Are you trying to kill me?" He sounds wounded and his eyes are closed as if in pain, but then laughter rumbles in his chest like an approaching juggernaut.

"I'm sorry. If you'd moved out of the way ..."

As I try to disentangle myself, I think my knee might have caught him in the goollies. He rolls over onto his knees and eyeballs me. "Another lesson tomorrow? It is necessary, I think."

"No, it really isn't."

"Yes, it is, *mon caneton*, if only to teach you how to stop!"

❄

"Tonight the two of us are going dancing," announces Gemma as we're clearing away the mess the lads have left behind. They've already headed off on some mad *stagscapade* to the neighboring town, so the coast is clear.

"Sure thing!" I'm looking forward to it. I love dancing, losing myself to the music, letting the beat hammer any doubts out of my head. And bloody hell, I could do with the release tonight. I told

Gemma about my skiing lesson with Mr Misery and she nearly fell on over, she was laughing so hard. I love this about Gemma. She's always laughing, and you know how they say laughter is the best medicine. It's also highly addictive.

"What did you get up to after I woke you up?" I ask.

"You what?"

"I hammered on your door because Leo was going mental."

"Oh, yeah." She stuffs her hands in her pockets and buries her nose in her coat collar.

"So?"

"So what?" she looks at me, and I swear there's a guilty glint in her eyes.

"You weren't in your room, were you? I wondered why you didn't answer. Where were you last night then, you dirty stop-out?"

"I was there. I just must have been in the shower or something when you knocked."

I'm not convinced, but I let it drop because we've reached Ava's, the only nightclub in town.

Inside is a heaving mass of bodies. We make a beeline for the bar to buy Mojijtos because it's still early enough for happy hour. But who do we see looking unhappy on the other side? Leo. What happened to him going out with the lads? Gemma grabs my hand and drags me along in her wake.

"Gemma! What perfect timing. I was just buying a round of drinks," says Leo, sarcastically, as if we've come along intentionally to take advantage of the situation. I'd like to turn around and leave, but I don't think they'll refund our entrance fee and Gemma doesn't even seem to notice.

"Thanks, Leo, I'll have a Mojito," she says.

"Valerie?"

Well, I'm not one to flout an opportunity. "Thanks, I'll have the same."

"Are the others here?" Gemma asks, shouting to be heard above the music,

"Over there."

I take a couple of quick photos of guys at the bar because I don't want to have to make conversation with Leo, and I don't want to forget to make Simon jealous. I catch Leo's eye and he gives me that look — the sad-cow-can't-leave-social-media-alone pitying look. I do my best to ignore it and pretend I'm oblivious and loving the buzz. But actually, it's my head and chest that are buzzing, mainly with anxiety, and because, well, Leo …

"Couldn't resist us?" growls a voice in my ear.

Can't resist him? *As if!* I whip around, nearly knock the tray of drinks Leo is carrying flying.

"La vache!"

And is he now calling me a cow? I'm in no hurry to follow, but I realize Gemma is making her way over to the guys and I don't want to hang out by myself looking like Billy-no-mates. Holding the tray aloft, Leo weaves his way through the throng and I reluctantly trail in his wake, resting the urge to give him a sharp shove in the back.

"It's our second lucky mascot!" shouts Josh, leaping to his feet and kissing me on both cheeks. This is a bit too pally for my liking, but I can see Gemma is doing the rounds so I feel I have to follow her example, until I get to Leo. He eyeballs me and I back away. This is one messed up work situation.

I pull Gemma aside. "I might go back!" I shout in her ear. "I don't think we're wanted."

"Nonsense! You don't mind us joining you, gents, do you?" Gemma yells with all the tact of a wrecking ball.

They all reply with words of encouragement to stay, except for Leo.

"I'm not leaving until I've got my money's worth," says Gemma. God love her. I want to curl up in a ball under the table, never mind whatever beer slops are down there. Leo is staring at me. It's very unsettling.

"Right, let's dance then. Come on." I grab her hand and pull her with me into the crowd, leaving the lads behind.

"That was a bit rude. What's got into you?" she asks.

"Nothing."

"Could've fooled me. You're dancing like a woman possessed."

"Maybe I am possessed. By the devil."

"Here, give me your camera then. I want Slime-on to know what he's missing."

"This!" I say throwing my arms up and nearly give a bloke behind me a black eye. Gemma creases up laughing and the bloke grabs me around the waist, twirling me round. I wink as Gemma takes another shot and then cringe when I spot Leo glowering at us both. What does it matter if he thinks I'm a total trollop? I'm not at work now!

I pocket my phone and keep shaking my booty. It's my own time and I'll do exactly what I please, thank you very much.

It's easy to lose track of time when you're drinking and dancing. A couple of hours or so later, I go back to our table to find Leo there, by himself. He's the only one of the lads who hasn't put so much as a toe on the dance floor.

I neck my drink. When I finish, I find Leo's eyes fixed stonily on me. "What?"

"*Bof.*" He shrugs. That seems to be a very Leo expression and gesture. That and the eyebrow twitch.

"*Bof*. Why d'you come if you don't like dancing?" I ask cheekily. I may not be entirely sober. I may need to tone down the aggression.

"What?"

I lean across the table and repeat my question.

"Who says I have any choice? And who says I don't like dancing?"

"Well, you haven't exactly been shaking a leg on the dance floor."

"Shaking a leg?" he stands up and comes close. He shakes his leg, and it's so comical, I can't help laughing. He's pretty tall as well, towering over me. "Would it make you happy if I dance, or do you just want the opportunity to take a photo of me making an idiot of myself?" asks Leo

"Chance would be a fine thing," I say.

For a heartbeat, I'm caught in his dark stare. For a heartbeat, my stomach squeezes and I stop breathing. Am I flirting with my boss?

He leans closer still. "Let's go then." He puts a hand under my elbow and steers me back onto the dance floor.

This is not what I wanted at all. The dance floor is packed and we're more or less crushed against one another. I feel horribly self-conscious all of a sudden, as if I've forgotten how to dance. Leo's hand dives into my jean pocket. What the heck? He pulls out my phone. "A selfie for your friends?"

I'm dazed, still somewhat shocked by the sensation of his hand fishing around in the pocket of my jeans. Leo holds my phone above us, hooking an arm around my waist and drawing me tight against him. In a couple of seconds, I'm reduced to a seething mess of jangling nerve-endings, hyperaware of the hard planes of his body and his hand on the bare skin of my waist.

"Look up, *mon petit diable*, and smile!"

The flash goes off. I smile too late. He slides the phone back into my pocket as if it's the most natural thing in the world. And somehow, we seem to be dancing face to face, his hand still on my hip. Holy hot hell! I have never wanted to do something quite so daft in all my life, as I now want to wrap my arms around his neck and press my thirsty body to his. But this is Leo. My boss. Who I do not even like. Is it possible to be crazily in lust with a man you dislike?

"What does *mon petit diable* mean?" I ask.

He places his other hand on my other hip and pulls me closer still. "My little devil." He murmurs more French in my ear — it could be a shopping list — but it's like my ear is hard-wired to my groin and my entire body turns to liquid fire. Not a good idea. My brain is malfunctioning. My feet turn to wooden blocks.

"Excuse me, I need—" I push him away and turn my back, diving into the crowd. Back at the table, I grab my coat.

"You're not leaving already?" says Benoit.

"Uh, yeah. I've an early start tomorrow. Tell Gemma I've gone back to the chalet, would you?" Without waiting for a reply, and without looking around because I most definitely do not want to see Leo. That man does inexplicable things to my body and he has the nerve to call me a devil. He's wickedness incarnate.

I make my way to the exit and into the biting fresh air. I sucking the air like I've been held underwater. What the holy heck was that all about? I cannot fancy Leo. It's one thing letting Simon know I'm having a fine old time without him, but not with my boss! That would be a serious case of out of the frying pan and into the fire. And I feel scorched. My throat is parched from all the shouting to be heard over the music. My face feels flaming hot. My groin is tingling. There was I thinking I would never so much as look at another man and wanted nothing more than to win Simon back, but my body apparently has a whole other agenda...where Leo is concerned.

I march along the icy street, furious with myself. I don't know what is going on with my messed up head, but I know Leo is no solution to the Simon problem.

Leo was playing with me like a cat plays with a mouse. A bloody big horny cat. I need to get some sleep. Go bury my head under the duvet and hope I wake up feeling sane in the morning.

8

VALERIE

So I've decided, I'm sticking this out. Leo may be a prize knucklehead, and it's quite possible last night he danced with me just because he thought it would be a lark, but I don't see why I should leave a job I enjoy — unless he sacks me, of course. That is still a possibility.

I have to keep things strictly professional and not do anything stupid like dance with him again. After leaving him stranded on the dance floor without explanation, I'm sure keeping my distance won't be a problem.

Gemma comes in looking as if she hasn't even had five minutes sleep. I plate up the fried eggs, bacon, sausages and beans.

"Thanks for waking me. Sorry, I'm late."

"No problem. What time did you crawl in last night?" I ask.

"Too late. Should've come back with you. Why didn't you tell me you were leaving?" she groans.

"Sorry. Did Leo say anything?"

"About what?"

"Oh, you know—"

I'm about to elaborate, but gales of laughter from the next room interrupt. Gemma opens the hatch and immediately starts hooting with laughter. "You've gotta see this!" She rushes out, but whatever it is, I really don't think I need to see it. Until I hear Leo.

"You cannot be serious!" he snarls.

Oh, maybe this is too good to miss.

"You *have* to. Rules are rules." I think that's Antoine.

"*Putain*. Fuck the rules!" snaps Leo. Okay, I can't ignore this any longer.

I peek through the serving hatch. It takes me a moment to compute what the guys are rolling around laughing about, and why they've stripped down to just their undies, but then I see Josh wriggling himself into a pink lycra stocking that does up over his head. Someone has brought morphsuits, those all in one lycra bodysuit thingummies. I cannot wait to see Leo in his.

"You have to wear it all day," says Antoine.

"I do not. I'm not going to be seen dead in that thing." Leo looks mortally offended. I guess his pride will not allow him to look less than perfect, even for five seconds. My brain flashes back to the packed dance floor last night. He was decidedly dishevelled and less than perfect then, but damn he was sexy.

"Yes, you do. Unless you want us to lose fifty points because you're too precious?" says Guillaume.

"What are you so razzed up about? It's just a bit of fun," adds Benoit.

"I cannot believe this. I have far more important things to be getting on with." A stream of French expletives (at a guess) fly from Leo's mouth. He tears off his t-shirt and jeans, looking thoroughly pissed off. His body is even more ripped than the army guys'. As well as being worked up, he clearly works out. But now he gets to look like a giant sperm along with the rest of them. Serves him bloody well right.

I can't help giggling and, of course, not one to miss a potential social media opportunity, I grab my phone. Priceless. I focus on Leo and snap a couple of shots, unable to suppress the snort of laughter that explodes from my nose.

Leo spins around.

I take another shot.

"Valerie!" says Leo, a hair-raising note in his voice.

I hastily close the serving hatch and hide my phone in the bread bin, unable to stop my snickering.

Leo appears in the kitchen doorway.

"Where is it?"

"Where is what?" I ask innocently. "Oh, don't you look lovely. Lycra suits you."

"Delete those pictures."

"Is that an order?"

"Yes." He bares his teeth at me. "If you want your skiing lesson today."

I'd forgotten about that. "Oh, I'm sure I can manage without. Maybe Gaspard will be free," I tease.

I cannot help chuckling as he stalks from the kitchen.

"Leo, I've never seen you looking so … erm … streamlined," says Gemma, as he stomps past her.

"Shut it, Gemma, or I'll streamline the two of you out of your jobs."

"What a bod!" she whispers entering the kitchen, flapping her hand as if she's very, very hot.

"But not man enough to wear lycra in public." I quip, possibly a little too loud. Checking the picture on my phone, it's impossible not to laugh at Leo looking like a raging bull — in red, white and blue lycra. How can I not post that to Instagram? But I catch sight of another photo, which stops me in my tracks. Leo and me dancing. I don't know whether I look more startled or terrified, but there's no denying Leo is smiling beautifully, nor that's he's appallingly good looking. Without stopping to think, I post that picture with the caption: *Taking the boss for a spin!*

9

LEO

Leo

As I make my way to the nursery slope. The only advantage to wearing this stupid morphsuit is no-one can recognize it is me inside it. However, there is an obvious disadvantage to skiing without the rest of the group because hanging out on the nursery slopes by myself in this outfit with all the kids here ... There are a few muffled sniggers, but more glares from concerned parents shielding their precious offspring from me. I definitely look like some sort of pervert.

Ignore them, I tell myself brusquely, squaring my shoulders.

Valerie is easy to locate. I hear a shriek and spot a skier veering off piste, before losing it and landing in a heap. *Ah, oui. Mon caneton.*

Wearily I make my way over, wondering why I am such a glutton for punishment, and why I let her jibe — *he's not man enough to wear lycra in public* — bring me away from my desk to prove a point. That and wanting to know why she disappeared in such a hurry last night. It bothers me that I overstepped the mark. It bothers me that I lost control at all. Today I need to reestablish the professional boundary between employer and employee. A conversation with myself starts in my head:

So how the hell are you going to do that, teaching her to ski dressed head to toe in lycra? Come on, lycra is almost the French national costume. Think of the Tour de France, all those lycra-clad men on bicycles.

In theory it should be possible, I try to convince myself. If only it weren't the nursery slopes.

"Valerie," I say, waving, hoping all those mothers are paying attention and know I have a good reason to be here. I make my way toward her and hold out my hand to help her up.

Brushing snow from her goggles and face with her mittens, she peers up at me in surprise. She reminds me not so much of a duckling as a mole like in the children's tale *Wind in the Willows*. From the expression on her face, I probably remind her of the Toad of Toad Hall — or, being French, the Frog of Frog Hall. I imagine she would rather like to feed me into a mincing machine.

Her face twitches, especially her eyebrows, which are outlandishly expressive. "What are you doing here, Leo?" she says, rubbing again at her goggles.

I grit my teeth. "I've come to teach you your ski lesson," I say, grabbing her hand and hoisting her upright, "and if you utter my name out loud once more, I am going to push you down a black run. Is that clear?"

She smiles. "Utterly."

Something about the tilt of her mouth and the sincerity of her tone makes me want to kiss her, but today I shall remain in control of the situation. And to be honest, she's bloody hopeless, struggling to even get her skis back on. I take matters into my own hands. Grabbing her leg, I line up her ski boot with the ski fastenings and apply a little extra pressure. Then we do the same with the other foot.

"There."

"There, there," she says brightly, like a mother comforting a child. She claps her hands together and bites her lip.

There, there? Be calm, Leo. Remember your good intentions. Keep control.

"I thought you weren't going outside today." She glances at my chest and lower. Does she imagine that just because she is wearing goggles, I'm blind to her looking me over and being so thoroughly amused?

"I finished my work. And I'm a man of my word," I growl.

"Oh good. I do like a man of his word. They are very few and far between," she says, digging her ski poles into the snow and setting off at snail's pace. "Take my ex for example…"

I watch her go. She's not elegant. She is most definitely infuriating. But, I have to admit, like a disaster you can see unfolding, I find it impossible to peel my eyes from her.

As I ski after her, I try to pinpoint what this compulsion of mine is, why I cannot keep away. It's nothing to do with her glamour, or style, or sexiness, though she is not unattractive. She is wholesome, fresh-faced and as natural as a newborn foal with her gangly legs splaying in all directions. There is a certain naivety and vulnerability about her that makes me want to protect her, perhaps.

"*Bah!*" I can't believe I am having such idiotic thoughts. I should leave right now. But also, something makes me want to prod around and investigate further. Peel off a few of Valerie's layers… *Merde*, there go any professional boundaries. And *quelle surprise*, Valerie has collapsed in an ungainly heap again.

❄

Val

After an hour, during which time I manage to stay on my feet because I'm no longer madly intimidated by Leo, especially not in his spermsuit, Leo suggests we get the chairlift up to the top of the *Blanchot* so I can have a go at a green run.

"If you're woman enough," he adds, almost as an afterthought. But not *almost* enough. He must have heard my comment about him not being man enough to go out in public in his morphsuit this morning. Oops.

"I'd love to," I say, because really what else can I say knowing that. Leo explains how to sit on the chairlift.

"Yes, I think I can manage!" I say breezily, but get a bit of a shock as the seat scoops me off my feet and lurches forwards. A little gasp escapes me.

"Put your feet on the bar," instructs Leo.

The skis are rather heavy and cumbersome and not so easy to maneuver. Leo grabs my dangling legs, helping to reposition them on the skids; his grip leaves me tingling. In fact, I feel slightly dizzy as the chairlift gains height. Is this the Leo effect, or is it the high altitude? I look at the ground a long way below and grip the hand rail tighter. Altitude. Definitely altitude.

For a while, neither of us speak.

And then we both try to speak at once.

"You go ahead," says Leo.

"I was wondering when you first learnt to ski," I say.

"Is that all?" He frowns. "To tell you the truth, I can't remember. Maybe as soon as I could walk. My parents were both keen skiers. That is how they met."

He falls silent again. The chair lift makes a slightly alarming screech and my grip on the handrail tightens. *No need to be alarmed. I'm sure this is normal.*

A dimple appears in Leo's cheek. I can't see his eyes because they're hidden behind ski glasses, and I could be wrong, but I think the bastard is enjoying my discomfort. I stare resolutely ahead, gritting my teeth, determined not to show I'm a bag of nerves, though the chairlift seems to be grinding to a stop which is enough to make my stomach plummet toward my ankles.

The sun goes behind a cloud.

"Is it normal for a chairlift to stop like this?"

"It happens. It's a great view up here, is it not?" asks Leo, inhaling gustily.

I try to focus on the mountain peaks ahead, not the drop to an icy death below, nor the fact that it's bloody freezing and it won't be long before we're turned into human ice lollies. But the blue sky, the odd cloud and jagged mountain peaks really are breathtaking. "Yes, it's very nice—"

The chair jerks forward two meters and stops again, making my heart explode in my chest. I grab Leo's arm and let go again. We are swaying twenty meters — it could be fifty or one hundred, who's counting? — above the ground, the wind picking up cutting through my thick down jacket.

"*Merde!*" says Leo, twisting around to look behind, making the chair lift bounce some more.

"Could you not do that!" I glare at him.

"Do what?"

"Make this bloody chair bounce! It's bad enough with the wind already."

"*Desolé.* Sorry. What are you afraid of? Is it the height? Do you think we shall plunge to our deaths?"

Well, now that he puts it like that... "No, I'm not afraid!" I'm terrified.

Cautiously, moving as little as possible, I try to peer behind to see what's happening. There's someone shouting and waving their arms in a typical French manner, and if I'm not mistaken, there's a flurry of activity which could be interpreted as an emergency.

"I'm sure we'll start going again in a jiffy," I squeak because my jaw is clenched.

"*Oui.* They'll sort it soon. What is a jiffy? I've not heard that expression before."

I suspect he's trying to distract me. "It's what my mum sometimes says. Old-fashioned. It means quickly, I guess, like in a flash, in a second."

"Ah. In a flash." His mouth quirks. Something else on his mind, perhaps.

The chairlift starts bouncing again. I glance at Leo. The cold is turning his mouth slightly purple now, his hands are in fists on his knees and his knees are bouncing. He sees me staring at his legs and stops. It's the cold, I tell myself, nothing to do with the fact that he's bricking it same as me. And seriously, Leo must be frozen solid in his skimpy morphsuit.

"You must be freezing," I say.

"*Bof*. If only I could retract my testicles up my backside like a sumo wrestler," he replies, totally deadpan.

A snort of laughter escapes me. "They do not!"

He grins. "They do. For sumo wrestlers it's a required skill, but sadly not one I've yet accomplished. I could warm us both up if you'd like."

"No, thank you!" I snap. "If you move, you might unbalance the chair and these wires, or whatever the hell we're suspended from, could send us crashing to the ground."

"That's not inconceivable."

"What?" I yelp, beginning to find Leo's company less than convivial.

He smiles at me ruefully, and despite the chill factor, my cheeks feel as if they are glowing.

"What now?" I demand, unable to contain myself.

"Nothing. I am simply trying to figure you out."

"Don't bother!"

Beside me, Leo chuckles. "I find you … interesting. May I ask, do you have a boyfriend? You mentioned an ex…"

"I'm not sure that's appropriate. That's private and you're my employer. I'm sure that sort of question is unethical."

"Absolutely. But at this moment, right now, I don't feel like your employer. It feels like we might be the last two survivors on the planet."

"You're not making this very reassuring, you know."

His lips quirk again. "You could take some photos for your social media. Maybe that'll take your mind off things."

Good idea. I carefully take out my phone and snap a few shots, including one of him before putting my phone away again.

"I had a boyfriend," I say, rubbing my thighs. "We split up. But I'm perfectly happy being single." I'm not sure I sound as convincing, or as perky and positive about it as I'd like to. "What about you?"

"Alas. No boyfriend, though in this outfit, perhaps soon."

I grin. "What about a girlfriend?"

He pauses. "No. I am too busy for all that." He waves a hand in the air. "Fuss."

"You'll have to make time then."

He looks at me. "As easy as that. Like flipping a coin. Maybe I don't want a girlfriend."

Not being able to see his eyes is disconcerting. "Right you are. We're both happy being single then. At least we have something in common."

"Bof!"

"Bof!" I reply in kind. *Bof*! I've no idea if it means anything, but it sounds so scathing and French. "Don't you believe me?"

His laugh reverberates through the seat of my pants. "I know you are trying to impress someone. If not your boyfriend, then who?" He nudges me with his elbow.

"Maybe my thousands of admirers."

"Of course, I would expect tens of thousands." He grins.

It could be just the cold, but without realizing we seem to be inching closer together, trying to eek out whatever body warmth we can from one another. "So, Valerie, tell me about your admirers, or maybe your family, I would like to know more about you and where you're from."

"Is this like an interview?" My teeth have started chattering in earnest.

"Perhaps. If you are going to continue working for me after this week, I need to know more," says Leo. He puts my hands between his and starts to rub them. Even though we are both wearing gloves, a surge of warmth spreads through me, not to my peripheries where I probably need it most, but instead right between my legs. How awful. How shameless. Leo would probably die of mortification if he had any idea what he was doing to me.

It's very distracting, but I manage to give him a potted history. Brought up by a single mother. One brother at university. Nothing much of interest. "What about you?"

He hesitates. "I'm not sure you need to know anything about me."

"Yes, I do. If I *agree* to keep working for you, I want to know who I'm working for. All I know is that you're some hotshot venture capitalist businessman or something along those lines."

Before he can tell me anything, a man appears below and shouts up at us. Leo shouts back and they have a conversation in French. I barely understand a word.

"There is a mechanical fault, but they're trying to fix it." Leo puts his arm around my shoulders. "I am not being inappropriate, okay, but it is important we keep each other warm."

"Right," I say, "but no trying to climb inside my ski jacket."

He laughs again and looks down at me through his ridiculously long lashes.

"So you were saying ... your family..."

"Ah, moi. My father was English. He's no longer... " he pauses, "in the picture. My mother lives in the Gers, in the south of France, as does my brother. And I have a younger sister, Amé, who's proving a real pain in the backside. What do you like to do in your spare time?" he asks.

"Baking. And ... writing. I'm an aspiring writer."

"Oh, well, my brother would say, you cannot be an aspiring writer. You either write or you don't."

"Okay, I write. But I'm more of a hobbyist."

"I should introduce you to Hugo. He's an author. And a lot nicer than me."

"Surely not," I tease.

He laughs again. "If you're not nicer to me, I might just steal your jacket and throw you off this chair lift."

"There are too many witnesses," I say.

It rather feels like we're flirting again, despite shivering with cold. Maybe my boss is not so bad. I rather like the additional warmth and reassurance of his arm around my shoulders. *To hell with it.* I snuggle in closer. I'm sure Leo is only thinking about my health and safety, but all sorts of mad ideas are zipping through my head. Up close like this, with him not wearing much more than a layer of cling wrap and smelling divine, it's impossible not to be affected.

"I have a proposition," says Leo.

"Oh really?"

He grins wolfishly and his legs start bouncing again. I put my hand on his thigh to still it and then, seeing his expression, tuck it quickly back under my armpit.

I know he's staring at me. When I look up, our eyes lock. His are so dark, and if I'm not mistaken, troubled too.

"So your proposition?"

"It is not *mine* exactly, and it is somewhat awkward," he says, and coughs. "I wondered … *Merde*! How do I put this? I wondered if you might be interested … hmm." He clears his throat. "How you might feel about having some fun… with me…"

With him? My cheeks are suddenly scorching, and I have to admit the idea is not entirely unattractive now I've got to know him a little. Leo is ridiculously handsome and not entirely without a sense of humour and let's not forget that body. We lock eyes and I desperately want him to kiss me. But he's not moving an inch. And he's also still my boss. And what the hell am I thinking even considering it?

I attempt to laugh. "I'm not saying no out of hand, but I don't think it's the most sensible idea I've ever heard. We barely know one another, and then there's the fact you're my boss, not to mention that there's not a whole lot we can do stuck up here."

From the look on his face, I may have misjudged everything. Again.

A bark of laughter escapes him, and he removes his arm from around my shoulders. "It's not like that. The sort of fun I'm suggesting is the kind of stag party … final fling … type thing—"

"I'm sorry?" I choke. "With you or someone else?"

"No need to apologize. And no, of course not with me. It is … with Josh."

Am I hearing this right? "Are you suggesting … let me get this straight … No, you tell me. Exactly what did you have in mind, Leo?"

I may as well have been struck by lightning. My impression of Leo has taken a serious dive. There I was, quite liking him, even considering having some 'fun' with him, but the signals I'm getting now are that this is not about him at all and probably never has been. I wriggle as far away from his as possible.

"Oh, you know..." he says, looking uncomfortable.

"No, I'm not sure I do. Why don't you explain."

The windchill is bitter and we're suspended God knows how many feet above the ground, but he looks ... almost ashamed. "The guys mentioned getting a strip-o-gram for Josh, but..." He clears his throat again and stares at the clouds.

I wait for his face to crack into a grin, but he's deadpan and his words twist like a hook in my gut. I'd like to slap some sense back into him. I cannot believe he's asking me to be a stripogram.

"It was an idea someone suggested, nothing more. Apparently it is common on stag dos. If you wanted to do it, I could pay you a week's salary for a couple of hours' work." He won't even look at me.

"Really! A week's salary for just a couple of hours. How very generous. And what did you have in mind for seducing Josh? A pole dance? A lap dance? A bit of casual sex. And is this with only Josh or anyone who wants to take a poke?" It's a struggle to keep my voice even. I take a few deep breaths and tighten my grip on the chairlift handrail. "Out of interest. Did you put this idea to Gemma as well?"

"No. I—"

"You thought I would be an easy target?"

"Not at all." He compresses his lips. "I imagine you are far from easy."

"Yes, whatever crappy impression you have of me is totally wrong! I am not easy!" I snap. The people in the chair in front of us turn around and state. I cannot believe the audacity of this man. The nerve!

In the distance, it sounds as if the engine running the chairlift has restarted. Thank the Lord.

"I apologize. I take it that's a no."

I wait for him to look at me again. "Yes, that's a no." If only I could stalk away. Instead, I hunch my shoulders and stare in the other direction, the freezing wind making my eyes water.

"I didn't mean to offend you."

"I cannot believe you thought I'd be desperate enough to agree! It's insulting!"

There's a lurch, and the chair lift starts moving. "Thank God for that!" I say. "I've had enough of skiing and ski lessons to last me a lifetime."

I glare at him. He looks frostbitten. Is he going to say anything?

Leo takes hold of his ski poles. "Get ready to dismount," he says stiffly. "Shuffle forward on the chair. Okay, go." A firm hand on the small of my back pushes me forwards.

Please don't let me fall on my backside in front of Leo. Please don't let me fall on my backside in front of Leo. I wobble around precariously before loosing my balance and landing in a heap.

Leo

Ah, merde! That went even worse than I envisaged. Perhaps I should have confided in her. I have my reasons. I have a plan. It is all going to shit.

"Get the hell away from me," she says when I go to help her up. "I wouldn't accept your help if I'd broken my bloody neck."

"If you'd broken your—"

"Leo, unless you want me to sue you for ... for harassment, or something like that, you'd better just piss off and leave me alone."

Her blue eyes are icy, but nevertheless awash with tears. She takes off her skis and stomps down the piste. I feel one hundred percent the heartless bastard she's labeled me. And that, my friends, is how to keep women at arm's length.

I ski to the nearest café and order a *vin chaud*. I need something like hot wine to warm me up. I am chilled to the marrow, and I doubt it's because of what I'm wearing.

Perhaps I should have mentioned my suspicions that Josh would only too readily betray my sister, but my scheming would hardly be likely to go down any better. Amé's far too young to get married, but Valerie is even younger. And look what I was prepared to do — throw her into the lion's den. I don't trust Josh. Memories of our father beating the living crap out of our mother, us three children curled up under the kitchen table, flashes before my eyes. I cannot let that happen to Amé. But I also feel sick thinking about the look on Valerie's face. I shudder. I should never have let those words spill from my lips! What in God's name was I thinking? Maybe I am more like my father than I like to admit.

I telephone my brother and tell him what's happened. He sounds bored. "Your problem is you have a self-destruct button, Leo. Don't worry, I think that is the only family gene you inherited from Papa."

"I wanted to throw myself off the chair lift. If I thought I was going to turn out like that bastard, I'd rather top myself now."

"So, I guess you seriously like this girl, heh? Your chalet woman?"

"As a friend. As an employee. Not in the way you are implying. I like her because she's decent. She is charming, but a little fragile and ever so slightly nuts."

"Like Mama then," says Hugo.

Our poor mother.

"Let's say, I feel bad I misjudged things." I tell him about first meeting her while she was cleaning in her bra and knickers. "And don't put that in any bloody book!" I say when he chuckles.

"It sounds like you are not immune to falling in love, Leo, no matter what you'd like to think. You've never rung me up about any of your other women before."

"Don't be fucking ridiculous. I'm not in love!"

There is a long silence. I look up and realize half of the café is looking at me. I get to my feet and walk outside.

"Leo, it's your life. You can choose what you want to do with it." He sounds weary. "But stop interfering with Amé's. I know you want the best for her, we both do, but Josh is not our father. And you need to let her make her own mistakes. How else will she learn?"

"*Bof.*" What I don't say is that my gut feeling that Josh is totally wrong for my sister was reinforced last night watching him with his arm around Gemma's waist helping her up the stairs. Admittedly, they were both very drunk and he wasn't being horrible to her, but let's not forget her room is on the ground floor. I can't help but remember how my mother used to help our father when he was drunk, the cruel things he'd say: she'd absorb it all, even the pounding of his fists, without a word. She made excuses for him. Until he nearly killed her.

I know this is a stag week, but … I cannot shake off the feeling that if this wedding goes ahead, Amé will not only be unhappy, but her love of life, her *joie de vivre*, will be destroyed.

I return to the chalet, my head a mess of thoughts: Josh is wrong for Amé. He is not good enough. She deserves better. And so does Valerie. *Mon Dieu*, how to make everything right?

Valerie makes herself scarce all evening. As I'm pouring everyone a nightcap, I see her slinking off quietly downstairs. Five minutes later, making my excuses, I follow her and knock on her door.

"Valerie, please may I explain?"

She opens her bedroom door and glares at me. "I don't care if you sack me. I think you're an unfeeling French pig and the answer is still no!" She slams the door in my face.

10

LEO

It's still dark outside when I wake up from a bad dream: my mother huddled under the kitchen table with us, but then she morphs into Valerie. Someone is rampaging around the house, throwing furniture and slamming doors, trying to find us. My father. Or is it?

I wake up with jolt, realizing that the only person making any noise is me.

My first coherent thought is, why is Valerie hiding from me? Then I'm hit by the Amé dilemma and how I keep her out of Josh's clutches, and finally work — my default. I'm behind on work. It's very unlike me. I need to read through the information I've been sent by the London office, but, sitting down at my desk, I can't seem to focus or throw off the weight of frustration and guilt. All I see is Valerie's horrified face on the chairlift, almost as pale as snow, or her slamming her door in my face.

I sit at my desk, and on a plain sheet of white paper, attempt to compose an apology. But though I want to make it right, I can't seem to find the appropriate words. I decide to come back to it.

I speak to a colleague in New York, and then I wander into the kitchen. The chalet is still silent apart from someone's snoring. It's

Matt. He's fallen asleep on the floor, his neck at an inhuman angle. Matt's in the other team. I could leave him well alone, but I grab a cushion and stuff it under his head, and then put a blanket over him. It must be the lingering effect of my mother on my mind. In moments of weakness, like the dead of night, I sometimes find myself remembering her small acts of kindness and miss her gentle touch.

The table is all set for breakfast. In the kitchen, the Tupperware boxes are stocked with food — no doubt Valerie's doing. There's a message on the side with instructions for tonight's supper. Of course, today is the girls' day off. I throw on a jacket and walk into town to buy fresh bread from my favorite all-night bakery. It's snowing and the dawn behind the mountain peaks is hidden by low cloud.

On a whim — maybe it's desperation — I buy a cupcake with a flower on it, deciding I'll give it to Valerie along with my apology. By the time I've got back to the chalet, this idea has developed into a full-blown breakfast delivery for outside her door.

Kicking the snow from my boots, I glance at the clock in the hall as I enter. It's now almost six. I wonder if the girls will lie-in on their day off. It's unlikely there'll be any skiing today because of the weather. I grimace, imagining the obligatory consumption of alcohol, which will happen instead. No matter. I start preparing a breakfast tray and then, not wanting to look as if I'm favoring Valerie, I make up a tray for Gemma as well. Unfortunately, I only thought to buy one cake. Too bad. That's for Valerie. I fill the trays with croissants, confiture, coffee (which will quite possibly be stone cold by the time they wake up), and on Valerie's I place the cupcake, wondering if I'm going soft in the head.

I'll just write an apology. I take off the cupcake and stuff it in my mouth because I don't want to give her the wrong impression and sentimental gestures are for fools. But I do leave the breakfast trays outside the girls' bedroom doors, praying they don't stumble over them half-awake and do themselves an injury.

I return to my room, my conscience slightly appeased, and settle to the business of proper work. I will write the apology later.

It's mid-morning before I hear the guys surfacing. Looking up from my laptop, the weather is not looking promising. I can't even see the town, let alone the pistes. I continue working until someone hammers on my door.

"Wake up, sunshine. Today is Team Treasure Day!"

Putain. I clench my fist in my hair. It's Antoine, and the day ahead sounds more like a Team Torture Day, not treasure.

I take my time before appearing. Making myself another coffee, I listen to their plans. There is to be a treasure hunt, various items and challenges for each team to accomplish, including each of us finding ourselves a Valentine's date for the following day, which — no prizes — happens to be Valentine's Day.

The very idea makes my toes curl. Yes, I've received a couple of Valentine's Day cards in my past, but I've never sent one, nor flowers, nor celebrated such a ridiculous concept.

"We need some impartial judges to make sure no cheating happens," says Harry (the only vaguely sensible one on Josh's team).

"I've already spoken to Gemma. She's game. She's going to work on Valerie," says Josh.

Valerie is sure to say no. I hope. I wander over to the dining table where they're lounging around, looking the worse for wear. Why are they planning to inflict more pain on one another? I fail to see the point.

"Leo, can't you *order* Valerie to participate?" asks Josh.

Is he still drunk? "*Euh, non.* It's her day off today. And even if it wasn't, I'm not about to force either of the girls to do something they don't want to do."

"Couldn't you be gently persuasive?" He grins. "Use a bit of that French charm. Whisper sweet French nothings in her ear like the other night on the dance floor."

I want to hit him again. There are other ribald remarks.

I give Josh the smile I reserve for idiots. "Believe it or not, Valerie is immune to my charm. Perhaps you should speak to Gemma. See if your English charm works any magic."

Josh gets to his feet. "That's a cracking idea, actually. I'll go and see her now. If they agree, then our team should be awarded the first bonus points."

"Whatever."

I'm surprised when he reappears ten minutes later. "They were very appreciative of the breakfast trays I gave them," Josh winks at me, "and they've agreed with one condition."

He is such a wanker. The idea that this man might one day in the not so distant future become my brother-in-law is hideous. "And what is the condition?"

"They get next week off. It was Valerie's idea. She mentioned you were staying on another week by yourself. Do you think you're up to looking after yourself for a whole week?"

As if I am too precious and pampered that I'm incapable of feeding myself! "Of course, that's hardly—"

"Great. I thought as much, so I agreed on your behalf. I also bagged Gemma for our team, so you've got Valerie. Bad luck, mate. She doesn't seem too keen on the prospect either. So chaps, let the games commence and may the best team win."

"May the best man win!" I mutter.

"Start time is midday. The girls are getting dressed and we just need to finalize the finer details of the challenge—"

"Hold on. I have a condition of my own. No morphsuits!"

11

VALERIE

Valerie

The lads have come up with the most ridiculous list of items for their 'treasure hunt' today: a girl's bikini, a pink bra, a train ticket to Marseille, a dozen macarons, a group photo on the climbing wall, the biggest snowman, a kiss from a barman, and so it goes on and on and on.

Josh and Gemma knock on my bedroom door, taking me by surprise.

Why have they brought me a breakfast tray? Why are they together? They look incredibly pally and conspiratorial. What madness are they hatching? A myriad of questions flew through my brain and Gemma was at her most persuasive, saying we could use today as a bargaining chip. I'm not sure why I buckled before the day has even started, but I thought about having to endure a second week under Leo's patronizing glare and thought that suffering one day in return for a whole week of peace and quiet seemed like a fair exchange. I was surprised Leo accepted our conditions though.

But for now, I'm regretting my hasty decision.

The day unfolds like a bloody nightmare. Only worse.

Gemma and I have dual roles: both judge and team mascots. Our feet are not allowed to touch the ground until we are returned to the chalet with all team tasks accomplished ... and just to add spice to the whole ugly experience I've been assigned to Leo's team. From the look on Leo's face — as if he's stubbed his big toe — he doesn't much relish the idea either.

But focusing on the positives, it's not like I'm going to be stuck on a chairlift with him. There is safety in numbers. And I'm smaller and probably lighter than Gemma, which means I'll be easier to manhandle around the place.

I try not to let my dismay show as I study their list of challenges. Is a day of humiliation worth a week's pay with no work?

Before I have really considered the matter, I'm ordered onto Benoit's back and carried piggyback out of the chalet. We set off behind the other team and diverge as we head toward the Olympic Centre to get our photo on the climbing wall. The others head into town.

It's a fair distance, but Benoit trots along despite the blizzard of snow in the air. "You're lighter than my Bergin," he pants.

"Oh, yay. What's a Bergin when it's at home?" I ask, wondering if a Bergin feels this sodding uncomfortable.

"A rucksack. An army haversack, you know, with straps."

"Oh, great." This is perhaps a pinnacle of my life, being compared with a rucksack.

As we approach a bench, Benoit hollers, Antoine circles back and I hop onto his bony back. If I thought Benoit was uncomfortable, Antoine is worse. A tall bag of jogging bones. Next is Guillaume, who smells of alcohol and cigarettes and who, if I'm not mistaken, has not yet had a shower. I'm full of wonder that he's married. Does his wife have to remind him to shower daily like a little child? But I'm very appreciative and grateful to Guillaume because he doesn't try to make conversation, and he gets me to the Olympic Centre doors before I have to hop onto Leo. The very idea makes me wince.

It's wonderful to be inside, out of the bitter cold.

I've never attempted a climbing wall. I've climbed a few crags in

Yorkshire, but scrambling up Brimham Rocks are not quite the same as this. With Leo glowering at the bottom, it makes me want to get to the top as quickly as possible, and I rather take to the first activity. Beating all the army lads, I receive my second accolade of the day, this time from Leo, who says I climb like a monkey.

Ugly duckling. Rucksack. Monkey. So admired.

Once we've had our photo taken and I've come down from that particular high, I find Leo waiting for me at the bottom with open arms. *Oh dear.*

Neither of us says anything. One of the others detaches me from my harness and Leo carries me in his arms to a nearby bench, both of us avoiding one another's eyes even though we are ridiculously close. He dumps me, turns away, and orders me to climb aboard.

A hot breath of anguish escapes me.

"Just get on with it, Valerie. Do you think I like playing mule any more than you enjoy playing monkey?"

Reluctantly, I clamber on. It's as if we fit together. His shoulders are broad and his hips lean. I hate myself for moulding myself to his back, but my senses are overwhelmed. Leo smells like fresh snow and the mountain air and pine trees. Clinging onto his shoulders, despite the thick down jacket he's wearing, his muscles ripple beneath my fingers as he moves and I'm hyper aware of his firm grip around my thighs. And oh, my, Leo's hair. His thick, dark locks curl from beneath his hat like the devil's own temptation begging to be touched. I want to tear the hat from his head and see what it feels like. I'm almost delirious with longing. The heavenly scent of him, the manly strength of him, and chuffin' hellfire... what is wrong with me?

The blizzard has diminished to a soft flurry. I close my eyes as Leo jogs back along the snowy path. I'm almost willing him to slip because I'm not sure how long I stand this and I'd like an excuse to shout at him again, anything rather than feel this horrible ache between my legs which is never in my wildest dreams going to be sated. Opening my eyes again, I realize too late that we've already passed the low wall where Antoine handed me over to Guillaume, and the other lads are running ahead looking in no hurry to swap over anytime soon.

"Shouldn't you have handed over to one of the others?" I wrap my arms tighter around Leo's throat because I feel like I'm slipping and he hefts me higher.

"Attempting to strangle me?" he asks at the same time.

"Tempting idea," I reply through gritted teeth.

Leo laughs, and the sound vibrates through his chest into mine. Dear God, my nipples feel like pebbles. Save me from this man. Save me from myself and my mad female impulses. I see the bench where Benoit handed me over to Antoine up ahead.

"Benoit, it's your turn!" I yell.

"Are you trying to burst my ear drum? No problem. I'm fine!" shouts Leo and we sail past the bench. The other lads wait, but when Leo catches up all he does is give them instructions: Benoit is to go and purchase the rail ticket to Marseille, Antoine is to find the pink bra and Guillaume the bikini. He gives them a couple of addresses of women he knows who might be willing to help and tells them to inform them that Leo sent them.

I laugh. Of course. Leo probably has multiple women just waiting for him to say the word.

"We'll rendezvous at Jake's Bar at the foot of the pistes as soon as possible, d'accord? Okay?"

The lads tear off.

"You're very quiet," says Leo.

"Yes, and that's how I'd prefer we keep it," I say. I bet they're not happy, his exes. I bet they're strewn like autumn leaves, trampled under his great big galumphing feet—

He starts jogging again.

"Where are we going now?"

"To get the macarons. I know a place."

Five minutes later, we're standing outside Daphné's Patisserie and a helpful soul opens the door for us and ushers us inside. Leo dumps me on a chair. "Don't let your feet touch the ground."

Is that what it would feel like having a relationship with Leo, like my feet don't have the chance to touch the ground?

"Hello, Valerie? What would you like to drink?"

"Do we have time?"

The look he gives me makes me gulp. "We're in no danger of losing," he says.

"A *chocolat chaud* then, please."

He goes to the counter and I watch, unable not to notice how the middle-aged lady behind the counter smiles at him as she boxes up every single macaroon (or macarons as Leo calls them) on the tray. It's way more than we need. Leo and the woman look suspiciously as if they're flirting with each other, although she must be twice his age. He returns smiling, with a tray holding two steaming cups and a bag containing two cartons of macaroons. "Drink up. You look as white as snow and we've only done the first challenge."

We drink in silence. The hot chocolate is delicious, rich and creamy, and not overly sweet.

"I can't believe I haven't found this place already. This is fabulous." I'm practically humming with pleasure.

His eyes meet mine over the rim of his cup. "There are a lot of places you probably don't know yet. Some hidden gems. I could..." He stops.

"What?"

"I could give you a map," he says, not looking at me.

My puffed up ego deflates again. I look around the shop to avoid being burned by his intense eyes. My synapses spark at all the beautifully decorated arrangements of treats, and the smell in here is sensational. Burtonbridge bakery is very basic and not very inspiring. I wonder if I could create somewhere like this. A cake shop. Doing my writing on the side.

"Penny for your thoughts?" asks Leo.

"My onions?"

He smiles wryly. "If you like."

"It's nothing but a fancy, a French fancy."

He raises an eyebrow.

"Not that sort of fancy!" I say, feeling myself blush. "I was simply wondering if I could bake cakes for a living and —"

The door flies open, a cold blast of air and snow gusting in along with Josh and Gemma.

"Hello," mutters Leo.

They don't spot us and hurtle straight to the counter. Josh puts Gemma down on the floor. On the floor!

Leo goes to get up, but I put a hand on his arm to stop him. Taking my phone out of my pocket, I snap a couple of photos of them, Josh with his hand on the small of Gemma's back, sliding into her back pocket.

"Busted. That's fifty minus points!" I say in a loud voice.

Gemma and Josh spin around gaping, and Josh snatches his hand from Gemma's pocket. I raise my cup to them and drain the contents, reminding myself that Leo had done much the same thing: put his hand in my pocket when he got out my phone in the nightclub. It's meaningless.

"À la fin! It's time we move on," growls Leo.

I clamber up on my chair with the bag of macaroons in my hand. "Okay, let's go donkey."

Leo gives me a wry smile.

Gemma is trying to jump back onto Josh's back.

"Good luck buying any macarons," says Leo as we walk past and out the door laughing.

We return to the chalet. My feet are briefly allowed to touch ground again. I dash to the toilet, while Leo goes off to 'hide our macarons'.

"You ready?" he asks, returning downstairs.

"I guess."

We swap places, me mounting the steps. For a moment, before turning his back, he stares at me. He raises his hand and lets it drop again. "About yesterday," he says.

I spin him around and launch myself onto his back. "Let's not go there. That's one place I don't want to go or even think about. Let's just get today over with."

12

LEO

Leo

We get to Jack's before the others. Valerie is perched on a barstool doing everything she can to avoid looking at me or having to make conversation. Her clothes are typical warm weather gear, but I'm struggling to tear my eyes away from her face and those extraordinary eyes. It's as if I'm under some sort of spell, fascinated by her, neither understanding and increasingly not questioning the undeniable fact that I cannot stop staring, and all I really want to do, what I desperately wanted to do back at the chalet, is to carry her to my bedroom.

Before I make a fool of myself, I leave her on the barstool with instructions not to move and go in hunt of the other items on the list. When I return nearly an hour later, Valerie is looking decidedly warmer and pinker and glowing, but the guys are still nowhere in sight. The only challenge I have not met is finding myself a Valentine's date. I buy us both another drink. Valerie beams at me. I think she might be warming to me, so why not?

"Valerie, you know we've been tasked with finding a Valentine's date for tomorrow evening."

She squints. "Yes. What of it?"

"I wondered if you'd be my date."

"Certainly not," she says. "I'm sure there are loads of other women you could ask. Besides, Valentine's Day is for people in love, which we most bloody definitely are not."

"Yes, but—"

"You do not have a romantic bone in your body, Leo Coultier. Not even a *leetle eency weency* cell," she says, taking the piss out of my French accent. "I on the other hand am a true romantic. I would not degrade the idea of Valentine's Day with another of your charades." She raises her glass in a toast to me. "Here's to happy endings," she says, "finishing this quest, or whatever you want to call it, and getting home in one piece." She winks at the barman. *Mon dieu*, Valerie is drunk.

"What are you drinking? How many of those have you had?" I ask, eyeing the red concoction in her glass suspiciously.

"Something unpronounceable and I've lost count. What matters is that they're very delicious."

I'm about to say more, but a hand clamps my shoulder. "Mission accomplished," says Antoine, dangling a pink lacy bra between us and grinning smugly. "How did you two get on?"

"Oh, like a house on fire," says Valerie with a hefty dose of sarcasm.

"*Oui*. I bought all the macarons in the shop. Josh and Gemma arrived after us, so they might find it difficult to find any macarons in this town, unless they ask Valerie to make some. Which, of course, she won't. Not if she wants to keep her job. Will you, Valerie?"

Valerie laughs so hard she nearly falls off her barstool. I have to prop her up again.

Antoine buys another round of drinks and Valerie shows no signs of slacking. Not long after, the other guys arrive almost on each other's heels. We're done. With the exception of the kiss from the barman. The guy behind the bar is young and handsome and keeps looking Valerie's way. The idea of him kissing Valerie makes me feel distinctly queasy.

"So we have everything except the kiss from the barman sorted," says Guillaume.

"I suggest we draw straws," says Benoit.

"You've not sorted that yet? What have the pair of you been up to all this time?" asks Antoine looking at Valerie and me as if we have been shirking in our treasure-finding duties. Valerie looks flushed and guilty, even though we have been doing precisely nothing, more's the shame.

A heated discussion between the four of us ensues.

"Oh God, I'll do it. I'll do it!" blurts Valerie. "It's only a kiss."

We all stop arguing and turn to look at her. "What? I like Freddie. The barman. Just don't forget to take a photo for Simon."

"Simon?" Who the hell is Simon? And she knows the barman's first name? They're on first name terms? Clearly, I left her here by herself a little too long.

Guillaume calls Freddie the barman over. The challenge is explained. The barman stops drying the glass in his hands and smiles a bit too appreciatively at Valerie, who is fast becoming the color of the red leather she is perched upon.

"Oh, it'd be my pleasure," says the guy.

It is not something I wish to witness. She's not prepared to be Josh's distraction, but she's happy to kiss some random barman? A barman, who she barely knows. He comes out from behind the bar rubbing his hands on his jeans. My fists clench.

Valerie turns to face him, her lips trembling, but her chin lifted. Her eyes catch mine — defiant — and my gut twists. Before I know what I'm doing, I've spun the guy around and I'm kissing his great hairy mustache.

"Yeurggh! *Dégage!*" He pushes me away, throwing his arms up, swearing colorfully at me.

I wipe my mouth and add a few of my own profanities. "Stop complaining. It was for a good cause." The others are falling around laughing. "Besides, she's already spoken for," I lie. "Did you get the photo?" I growl at Antoine. He nods his head, but can't speak for crying. The guys are like kids unable to stop laughing. Benoit is actually rolling on the filthy floor.

Even Valerie is laughing. "That was almost chivalrous, Leo ... I didn't expect you, of all people...your face..." She cannot finish. She has to wipe her eyes, she's laughing so hard at me. Me! I don't see what's so funny.

"Right. Do you want to win this challenge or not? Let's go," I mutter, stalking toward the door, not waiting for anyone. I cannot go anywhere near Valerie. If I do, I might do something to jeopardize the fragile bond which today has built between us. Like kiss her. That's what I'd like to do. Kiss her, just to shut her up.

Five minutes later, out in the frigid air, which does little to pacify my hot anger, I glance over my shoulder and see that Antoine has Valerie thrown over his shoulder as if he's rescuing her from a fire. I guess he is, in a sense. The desire to touch her has reached fever pitch inside me. I feel hot and irritable and extremely uncomfortable. However, this is meant to be a team effort after all, so I slow my pace.

"You okay?" I hear Benoit ask Valerie as they swap over again.

"Oh aye, I'm champion. Remind me, what I'm getting out of this humiliation?"

"The *honor* is not enough?" asks Benoit, grinning cheekily and putting on a bad French accent.

"Honor my left foot."

Benoit laughs and starts the uphill trudge to the chalet. I decide to wait.

"If I puke ... down your back ... is that extra points?" asks Valerie as they pass.

She's not complaining as such, but she's looking a bit gray-faced.

"Put her down on this wall. She needs a rest," says Antonie.

"We can carry her like it's a log race," suggests Guillaume.

"That's a great idea!" agrees Benoit.

I roll my eyes. It is a terrible idea, but I bite my tongue. The guys are now treating Valerie as if she is precious cargo, admiration clear in their eyes, and why, just because she can climb a wall like a monkey, and offered to kiss some random barman, and has suffered all the humiliations today can offer without complaint? I don't know why the idea of their affection is making me so hot under the collar.

They fashion a sling out of our jackets. Valerie is instructed to lower herself carefully onto it but, of course, manages to miscalculate and ends up doing a back flip landing on the other side in a snowdrift. There are more drunken guffaws.

"Strictly speaking, I don't think my feet touched the ground because I'm on a snowdrift," says Valerie giggling and brushing herself off. She looks adorable with snow in her hair, her eyes shining, her cheeks pink, smiling happily.

"Come on!" I say. "We're wasting time."

"You'd better do the honors then," says Benoit. "It's your turn anyhow."

Valerie is picked up and manhandled by the rest of them onto my back.

"You're always like a bear with a sore head," mutters Valerie into my neck.

What? All I know about being a bear is that I have to grit my teeth and *bear* this. *Bear* the feel of her soft breasts pressed against my shoulders, *bear* her light breath at my neck and the feel of her thighs in my hands. It's a good thing I'm struggling up the steep climb back to the chalet and the weather is extremely cold because my twitching dick is forced into hibernation.

I open the door to the chalet with one hand. Valerie slips toward the doorstep and collapses in a heap on the threshold. She looks up at me, her eyes definitely unfocused.

"You know Leo, you might be a grumpy git, but you're the best ride," she giggles.

Oh man. Oh man. Save me from this woman. I am beguiled by a totally naïve, totally English, totally impossible girl. I turn away lest even in her drunk condition she sees what she has reduced me to.

"We still have a snowman to build," I say to the guys.

It's a mad scramble. The other team has still not appeared, but we're more or less finishing when Guillaume shouts, "Watch out! Here comes Josh McPosh!"

Before we know it, we're being pelted with snowballs. There's some fairly heavy duty squabbling in the garden as I vent some of my frustration on the other team and we all try to protect our snowman.

"Enough! Enough!" Gemma shouts from the doorstep.

The two girls stand arm in arm in the doorway. They couldn't be more different. Gemma is tall and strong and athletic. Valerie is propped up by her friend, but my breath catches in my throat at the sight of her. I want everyone else to disappear, so only I can take care of her.

"You'd better come inside before someone gets maimed. Valerie and I will look at all the evidence and declare the winning team."

"Well, clearly, it's the French team," says Valerie, God rest her inebriated soul.

"How's that?" Gemma removes her arm.

"Well, do you have any macarons? *Macarooooons*?" She squints at Gemma.

"Macaroons. Well…" Gemma looks at Josh. "They'd sold out."

"And we have evidence of a little slip up, don't we, Gem?" A teasing note has entered Valerie's voice, and Gemma looks taken aback.

"No-ohhh?"

Valerie thrusts her phone in her friend's face. "Feet on the floor. And you don't have so much as a snowball, let alone a snowman."

Gemma's mouth opens and closes. I guess she's not often bested by her friend. But then the pair of them erupt into helpless laughter clutching on to one another for support.

"Ah, buggerations. I have to be honest," says Gemma, looking at her team apologetically. "Josh I—"

"No!" shouts Josh, rushing over to her and trying to clamp a hand over her mouth. It's all looking rather intimate.

"Leo's team are the winners," Gemma laughs through Josh's fingers.

"Ah, fuck," Josh concedes and pulls Gemma into his arms.

I do not have time to feel smug. I also make a big mistake. Enormous. All my team are dancing about, cheering and chanting they're the winners. I am infected by the high spirits. They each give Valerie a friendly hug and a kiss on the cheek. Without thinking, I step up for my turn, clasp her face between my frozen hands and ... suddenly realize what I'm doing. But I don't stop. I cannot stop.

The world fades to blizzard as my lips touch hers.

13

VALERIE

Why did he have to go and kiss me? I was doing fine until then. I'd even managed to convince myself that Freddie, the barman, was right up my street. Now all I can think about is Leo's lips on mine, and how despite feeling befuddled with alcohol and then numb with the freezing cold, his mouth sent a shaft of heat through me, effectively blowing a fuse in my brain.

I can't stop thinking about him. The grumpy arrogant French git. I can't stop recalling those small rays of light: dancing together, or when he was helping me up from my wipeout in the snow, or even when he was charming someone else like that woman in the patisserie, or when he stepped in for me and kissed the barman. That image has me grinning again. But I have to face the facts. Leo is not interested in me. Simon was not interested in me either. I have to stop fooling myself as far as men are concerned.

Today, the weather looks perfect for skiing, but there's no way I'm going out on those slopes. I lie in bed until I've heard everyone rise, have breakfast, and troop off from the chalet, and then I creep upstairs.

I clear up the mess left behind from breakfast and put on some soothing music. I run a cloth over the sinks in the bathrooms, replace empty toilet rolls, make beds and return to the kitchen. Now I have a clear day ahead of me for baking and cooking because tonight of course is the lads' so-called Valentine's Dinner. Though, having heard all the tales of them finding their dates, there's nothing much romantic about it. Josh has asked Gemma, purportedly because that's his safest option being engaged, but the way those two have been looking at one another lately I can't help wondering if maybe Leo asked her to 'have some fun' with Josh. Surely, she wouldn't.

Pushing disloyal thoughts aside, I focus on the cooking. There's enough to keep my mind busy this morning, and I want to make the meal special. I might take some photos. This could be the start of a whole new cooking and baking career for me. The idea warms me ... like Leo's kiss. *Stop freakin' thinking about him!*

Instead, I visualize the French delicacies I saw the day before at the patisserie café and have a mind to attempt making. I plan the menu: roquefort and pear *galettes* for starters; *cassoulet* for main course; and chocolate profiteroles and a *tarte tatin* for dessert. First, I have to make the usual tea time cake for when the hordes arrive back from a day rampaging on the slopes. After that's done, I'll go into town to buy everything else.

I whip up a Victoria Sponge, put it in the oven and turn around to find Leo in the doorway. "Jesus!" I leap a foot into the air.

"Sorry, I didn't mean—"

"What the heck!"

I bite my tongue. This is *his* chalet. I am *his* employee. I need to wind my neck back in. "You surprised me. I thought everyone was skiing. What do you want?"

There is a stomach-swooping pause. Leo looks at his hand on the doorframe. He seems to be deliberating.

"The answer is still no, Leo." At least I sound calmer than I did the day before.

"I haven't even asked you a question yet."

"Well, if it's anything to do with Josh, or a Valentine's date this evening, I'm not the person to talk to." I fold my arms. "Or was it something else?"

"Yes. Can I be of assistance here?"

I nearly smile. "What were you thinking of doing? Beating a few eggs?"

Leo spots my scribbled shopping list on the counter, picks it up and waves it at me. "Are these for tonight?"

I nod.

"I could go and buy these things for you? Save you some time."

I consider for a moment. Why is he being so nice? I have no idea. What I do know is it would save me slogging into the *supermarché*. "Okay. If you're sure you're not too busy, I'd really appreciate that."

After he's left, I'm in even more of a spin. What is Leo up to? He must have a reason, surely? It can't be *just* because he wants to be helpful.

He returns laden with bags of shopping an hour later. I thank him and expect him to go, but he's still lingering by the kitchen door.

"Are you hungry?"

"Famished."

"If you're not going skiing, I'll make you some lunch and bring it through."

I make sandwiches for us both, and whip in and out of his room as quickly as possible. Being near him unnerves me. It's like my body wants to trip me over. Best keep a safe distance.

"Okay. I'm going skiing," says Leo through the kitchen door, half an hour later. "Would you like to come?"

"No, thanks," I say, not looking up.

Once he's gone, I allow myself to relax and focus on cooking again. I set the table for sixteen guests. It's going to be a squeeze, but it's not like this was my idea. I keep to the French theme and pray that if the lads pick up any French women for tonight, they're not highly critical of my attempt at their cuisine.

My choux pastry for the profiteroles is beautiful and light, and the *tarte tatin* looks glossy and utterly delicious. It takes all my willpower not to help myself to a slice. I'm excited at the thought of how happy everyone is going to be when they taste my food tonight. Profiteroles and *tarte tatin* done, I make a start on the cassoulet. I'm delighted with how well that's turning out too. It looks scrumptious and perfect for this winter weather. Admittedly, it doesn't look the most elegant in this enormous pot, but when I serve it, I'll add some garnish and attempt to make it look as appetizing as it does in the recipe book. Finally, I make a start on preparing the galettes. All I have to do is pop them in the over to half bake them. That done, I go into the sitting room to change the music and notice we're running short on firewood. Grabbing the wood basket, I nip outside to the terrace.

It's bitterly cold. I load up the basket and carry it back to the door and almost bang my head. The door has closed behind me. Not only closed, locked.

Oh damn! I go around the house rattling all the other doors, the wind piercing my jumper, my fingers starting to feel numb. Even worse, I can imagine my galettes in the oven turning a bitter shade of brown and my beautiful, delicious cassoulet bubbling away on the stove. It's enough to make any grown woman weep. All that effort going to shite.

Shivering, I phone Gemma. She doesn't pick up because no doubt she's still skiing, but I leave her an urgent message and text her as well. And then I do the only other thing I can think of: I call Leo.

14

LEO

Leo

By the time I get back to the chalet, Valerie is huddled in a corner against the wall, her arms around her knees, her teeth chattering like clackers. She looks colder than when we were stuck on the chairlift.

I open the front door, wrap my jacket around her shoulders and pick her up. The sour stench of burning drifts down the stairs. "Put me down," says Valerie. "I'm not injured."

She runs upstairs, and I follow. Turning off the hob, she peers into the pan. "Oh, no! Oh hell. It's ruined and I've destroyed your pan!" Tucking her hands under her armpits, still shivering, her eyes fill with tears.

"Forget the pan. I'm more concerned about you. Come here. You look frozen." I pull her toward me and rub her arms.

"What the hell am I going to feed everyone tonight?" She looks up at me with pain in her eyes. "I'd planned a special French meal and now we only have dessert. That's the one thing we could have bought!" Her voice warbles and her head droops to my chest.

"Hey, look at me."

Enormous watery eyes look up.

"No one is going to starve. We can improvise. Besides, I make a mean Pasta Carbonara."

She swallows and, half-laughing, steps away from me. "That's not very bloody French!" She wipes her eyes with the heels of her hand. "God, I'm so sorry. You must think I'm such a useless cow. What an idiot, locking myself out. Does this mean my job is…" Her chin wobbles. If she starts to cry, it will undo me completely.

"It doesn't mean anything. It's easy to forget to flip the catch on that door. But I do think you should go and warm up. In fact, I insist." I'd do it, but I don't trust myself to keep control of my baser instincts.

She shrugs out of my jacket and hands it back to me.

"I'll sort everything in here. You go and have a hot shower. The others should be back soon."

"If you're really sure."

"I'm really really sure."

Valerie takes one more glance at the pan, grimaces, and touches my arm as she leaves. It's a small gesture, but I can't stop thinking about it as I scrape the charred remnants from the pan. The pan is beyond saving, and maybe so am I. I can't get Valerie out of my head. Her upturned face and downturned lips. The feel of her nestled against my chest. Her light touch on my arm. Her trusting eyes. And the horrible sensation that it's me who has burnt the pan. I chuck it in the bin.

No-one mentions the slightly acrid smell in the air that evening. No-one else even seems to notice. All the guys have succeeded in finding dates, bar Josh who claims that as he's getting married, it would be inappropriate and therefore he's claimed Gemma as his 'safe' date for the evening. There's not much safe about Gemma. She's a tour de force who could give any of these guys a run for their money. I think of asking Valerie if she wants to be my other half for the evening again, but immediately dismiss the idea. She's withdrawn, hiding away in the kitchen, only smiling when someone compliments what's left of her food.

When I help clear plates after the starter, the conversation doesn't falter and I doubt anyone notices me go, except Gemma, who comes in after me and raises an eyebrow when I shoo her back out. "You go and enjoy yourself. I'm giving Valerie a hand with the pasta."

I don one of the aprons.

Valerie has already magicked up some homemade pasta, which I think is something of a feat in itself, and I rustle up a carbonara sauce. After that is consumed, there's lots of admiring noises about the delicious desserts even from the French women. The conversation is loud, the lads full of the day's skiing and the joys of Méricoeur, and generally trying to outdo themselves in front of the women.

I sneak back into the kitchen where Valerie is making coffee.

"Everything okay?" I ask.

She looks over her shoulder. "Absolutely fine. Really good actually, thanks to your pasta. Go and join the others."

"They're talking about going into town once dinner his done. What about you?"

She sighs. "I don't think so. I need some peace and quiet. It hasn't been the best day, I suppose. You know, I was looking forward to this evening, not to be out there, but because I had all these big cooking plans... That'll teach me to get too big for my boots, won't it."

"Don't let one mishap derail you. It's good to have plans. I have one of my own."

She doesn't answer, just pours cream into a small jug. I take cups out of the overhead cupboard and place them on the tray alongside a plate of chocolate truffles. I steal one and pop it in my mouth. "These are delicious. Divine!"

We lock eyes, and her cheeks suffuse with color.

"Did I tell you what a great cook you are? When you're not busy locking yourself out of the house." It's not easy to speak with a mouthful of truffle.

"No." A smile pulls at the corner of her mouth. "Stop being nice to me. I'm a walking disaster and you know it."

"Everyone is entitled to a few mistakes."

"Even you?"

"Especially me."

We can't seem to tear our gaze away from one another. She looks so crushed, I desperately want to close the gap, fold her in my arms and reassure her that everything will be just fine. It also might be that I'm selfish and need to reassure myself that I haven't totally ruined things between us.

She pushes the tray toward me. "If you want to be helpful, would you mind carrying these through for me?"

Fuck, I should have kissed her. Sighing, I take the tray and walk out again.

15

VALERIE

Valerie

After the success of the Valentine's meal — all thanks to Leo for saving the day — everyone heads into town for another night of dancing and drinking. Once I've heard the door slam, I go back upstairs thinking I'll just set the table for the morning. But the empty sitting room is not quite so empty after all. Leo is in there talking to someone on the telephone. I clear away the debris around him and, one-handedly, because he's still talking on the phone, Leo helps.

I guess, I'm thawing toward him. He is entitled to make mistakes like everyone else and he's not the ogre I imagined. He's actually been more considerate than anyone, Gemma, included. She seems very wrapped up in helping the lads have a great time, which is all well and good, but at the dinner table, she was getting very carried away even talking about joining the army. All that military banter must have gone to her head. I suppose it wouldn't be such a terrible idea *for her* — she's definitely always been a bit of a Wonder Woman — but I hate to think of her putting her life on the line.

Leo finishes his conversation and comes into the kitchen.

"I've got this, thanks," I say. "You'd best go after the others."

"*Bref*. I want to help. I do not want to go after the others." He stacks plates into the dishwasher, and I go to wipe down the table, avoiding being anywhere near him, tidying things up as best I can with shaking hands. I'm such a coward. I know I'm delaying going back into the kitchen, but I can't cope with being in such proximity to Leo. When I'm too close, my hands literally twitch at my sides, desperate to cling on to something. He's so outside the realms of potential boyfriend material that it's not even funny.

Leo appears. "Is there a problem?"

"No, um, I was just making sure it's all tidy in here."

"It's perfect." The look he gives me makes my stomach swoop. "I want to show you something. If you're not too tired."

"What sort of something?" My voice is jittery with nerves.

"It involves a walk and a drive. You up for that? It might improve your day."

"That wouldn't be difficult."

It's ten o'clock in the evening. If I was being sensible, I'd be heading for bed. Alone. But I don't really want to be alone. And I don't want to join all the others. And Leo is looking at me with hope in his eyes and a crooked smile on his lips.

"Okay."

"*Fantastique!*" His smile broadens and his wicked dimples flash. "You need warm clothes. Grab a jacket, and I'll meet you by the front door."

Rather than heading down the road into town, Leo takes a left, as if we were going out of town, but then we cut through to another road heading away from town down a dwindling lane. Leo leads me by the hand up to an old farmhouse and knocks on the door. From somewhere behind the building, dogs start barking.

"What is this place?" I ask.

"Belongs to my uncle. Jean-Luc."

A white-haired man comes out and they hug and kiss one another's cheeks. Jen-Luc takes us around to the side of his house where, under a lean-to, there are a couple of skidoo snowmobiles.

"Enjoy!" Jean-Luc gives Leo a hearty pat on the back and disappears back into his house.

"Ever been on one of these?"

"Never."

Leo pull-starts the engine and climbs on board. "Hop on behind. Let's go for a proper ride." He hands me a helmet and turns on the lights.

Once I've put my helmet on, like an eager child, I clamber on behind Leo. He takes my hands and wraps them around his middle. "Keep your feet on the footrests and hold on."

The sensation of flying through the night, the growl of the engine beneath my legs, the reassurance of Leo's broad back in front of me, the snow gilded by moonlight all around, is magical. Leo follows a track away from Méricoeur and all the houses. The gradation of the hill steepens, and I have to hold on tighter. Every skid sends my heart skittering.

Finally, the slope plateaus out, and we come to a stop. Stretching ahead of us is a breathtaking view of the valley, the twinkling lights of Méricoeur in the distance.

Leo turns off the engine, and I take off my helmet. It's so quiet. The air so pure it's sharp in my lungs. Stars glitter overhead, and my body tingles. I get off the bike and try to absorb it all.

"Pretty good, huh?"

Leo is smiling. Beaming, in fact. And the snow lit by the moon behind him makes him look unreal... I have to turn away. He looks like an angel. Or a god. Certainly out of this world. I cannot help but smile and hug myself because the thought that I'm possibly standing on the Alpine equivalent of Mount Olympus crosses my mind. I have no words to describe him or the view. "Pretty good," I repeat.

"I used to come up here as a kid, especially in summer. Jean-Luc is a farmer and there are some shepherd's huts even higher than this that we'd camp out in."

"It's incredible," I say, slowly recovering some of my sanity. "What a childhood you must have had."

"*Ah, oui.* And also ah *non*. It was no walk in the park, that's for sure."

"Oh?"

"Hmm."

He doesn't seem keen to say any more, so I let it go and instead focus on savoring the moment. I'd take this over a Valentine's dinner date any day. I think about taking out my phone and trying to capture it on camera, but I could never do it justice. It would look black with a few specks of light. Besides, I think I'm over trying to impress Simon. Right now, it's all rather surreal, but I think I'd rather impress Leo.

"Thank you for bringing me here. It's magnificent." I turn to look at him, to find him staring right back. Feeling slightly awkward, I stare at the carpet of stars overhead. "It really is like a winter wonderland."

"Valerie."

I look at him again.

"I have..." He pauses, and then casually brushes a strand of hair away from my face. I go to tuck it behind my ear and he clasps my hand. "What I wanted to ask earlier. How would you feel about spending the day with me tomorrow?"

My heart swells in my chest. It might explode. I don't want to show how giddy the prospect makes me, but I can't stop from smiling. "That would be champion."

"Ah, yes, champion. We are the *champions* of the world up here." He pulls a flask out of a compartment on the snowmobile and unscrews the lid.

"Are you taking the mickey out of my Yorkshire accent?" I ask.

"I wouldn't dare," he says.

It is taking me a while to figure out Leo's sense of humor. It is so very dry. So dry that it is making my throat parched. When he offers me the flask, I accept eagerly.

It's a hot spicy *vin chaud*. Licking my lips, I hand it back to him and watch him take a swig. It's quite some profile.

We pass the flask back and forth, the alcohol warming me from the inside. The world is hushed, except for my heart, which is pounding like the drums of war. I can't stop stealing glances at Leo's face, which in this light seems both mysterious and exquisitely, painfully attractive.

Without breaking eye contact, Leo screws the lid on his flask and puts it away. He steps toward me, takes hold of the front of my jacket in both his hands, and draws me closer still. "Now is the time to object, before I do something really inappropriate," he whispers.

"What sort of inappropriate?" I'm unable to move, mesmerized by his dark eyes and desperate for him to kiss me. I'm not sure who closes the first, but our lips meet. His kiss is as soft as freshly fallen snow, his breath sweetened by the wine, his tongue a key that unlocks every inhibition. But it's achingly brief. "I've been wanting to do that all night," he says.

"Really? Just that?"

A huff escapes him. "Not just that." And he kisses me again, ruthlessly. I cling on to him — it's that or let my knees buckle and slide to the ground. His tongue triggers pulsations of heat in my core. He tastes of wine and wickedness. He pulls away again and studies my face. So serious. So gorgeously grumpy.

"You can smile," I say.

The smallest smile tweaks at his mouth. "Sometimes when I'm near you, especially with those other guys around, smiling feels challenging."

"Just so long as this wasn't one of your stag party challenges!" I joke, completely destroying the moment.

"*Bof!*" He lets go of me and steps away. He doesn't actually deny it, and I'm left feeling shaken to my core.

Hold on, was that a dare?

"We should go back," he says. "You're getting cold, *n'est pas?*"

16

VALERIE

I spent most of last night cursing myself for blurting out the first thing that had come into my head and destroying my moment with Leo and in a cold tangle of sheets that I'd been played. His kiss was a dare. When we got back to the chalet, everyone else was back, playing some sort of drinking game in the sitting room from the sound of things. In a panic, I whispered thank you and goodnight and rushed straight to my bedroom. The last thing I wanted was to face an interrogation about where we'd been, or what we'd been up to together. Or to listen to what Leo told the lads.

This morning though, it's as if nothing ever happened between Leo and me. No-one mentions a thing, so perhaps he's said nothing. Yet. Everyone is getting ready for the last day's skiing, Leo included. I momentarily catch his eyes, but he turns his back on me.

Last night felt magical; but maybe not to him. If it wasn't a dare, he might be regretting our kiss. He is my boss after all. Shit, perhaps it was a test? Maybe it was the excuse he was looking for to sack me. Was it my fault? He'd said something about it being inappropriate hadn't he? Or maybe it really was just another stag party challenge. Inside my head is like being inside a tumble dryer on full spin.

"What are your plans, today?" asks Gemma, yanking me back to the present. "The weather's looking fab."

My plans. I can't help but think about my conversation with Leo from the night before. What are my plans? Usually I'd be thinking about what I could post on social media, or what cake I would bake, or what scene I'd write that day. But my mind is blank. It's a bit like trying to act normal in a snowstorm.

I look outside the window. Incredibly, the sky is a vivid cobalt blue. A perfect for skiers... or lovers. "I'm not sure. I might chill out here."

"You can't waste a day like this. You've got to get out on the slopes!"

Of course, I think again of Leo. Leo, Leo, Leo. Him teaching me to ski. The two last people on earth on the mountain top last night. But the last thing I want him to imagine is that I'm some lovelorn loser, hanging around waiting for another skiing lesson from him.

"Valerie, you really need to get out! It's not good for you being stuck inside all day, especially not on a day like this," insists Gemma. She seems pretty determined to get me outside and force me to enjoy myself. "I mean, think about the photos you could take today. Make Simon jealous."

Leo is passing by the kitchen. His eyes flick our way, but then he's gone.

I should tell her I don't give a damn about Simon any more. "I'll probably go for a walk once I've done the cleaning and made this cake. You go. I'll finish here."

"Make sure you do," she says, giving my arm a friendly squeeze. "Text me to let me know when you're going out. I'll be checking."

"Yes, Mummy!"

I busy myself getting the ingredients for macarons out of the cupboards. I've a mind to try my hand at them. I try to summon images of Simon to my head, but all I can see is Leo. It's crazy. The desire to see Simon, or talk to him, or even know what he's up to has vanished. Poof! My feelings for Simon seem to have melted into a muddy puddle I wouldn't even step in with welly boots on. It should be a relief, but I'm cured of one man, only to fall for another. I'll tell Gemma soon enough, but I'd rather wait to have that conversation when the guys have left and we have a bit more time to ourselves.

Everyone leaves the house, including Leo, and my heart squeezes with disappointment. How is it that I can't summon up the energy to care anything for Simon any more and yet there's this aching sense of loss for Leo when he only stepped out of the door five minutes ago? Maybe it's a rebound thing, I tell myself. Maybe I'm fickle. Maybe I'm so desperate that a few crumbs of attention have gone to my head.

The next half hour is spent cleaning the house and rebuking myself for developing feelings for someone out of my league. He no doubt has dozens of women in Méricoeur he'd rather spend time with, and he remains, let's not forget, my boss. I can't help replaying the moment I first saw him standing in the bedroom doorway, me in my knickers. I look up, hoping to see him here, but of course, he's not.

My phone pings with an incoming text, my stupid heart leaps, but crashes when I see it's only Gemma.

> You dragged yourself from the house yet???

I sigh. I probably should do something physical to take my mind off Leo. I need to squash the spark which keeps telling me he might turn up for another ski lesson.

I text Gemma back.

> Nearly done. Going out in five minutes, I swear! x

I'm so fed up with myself for holding on to this shred of hope. Fed up with Leo for not feeling how I do. Fed up with the world for looking so bright and bloody beautiful when I'm miserable.

I stomp into the kitchen to take the cake from the oven, only to find Leo with it already out, stealing a corner flake.

He straightens up looking decidedly guilty. "*Oooh la la!* Busted."

I laugh. I want to run up and hug him. "What are you doing back here?"

He sinks his hands into his pockets and hunches his shoulders. "I ... I guess I came to find you."

I put away all the cleaning things and wash my hands in the sink, taking my time, hiding my enormous grin. "Whatever for?"

"Whatever for?" Oh God, he's behind me. "Didn't we plan to spend the day together?" He murmurs in my ear.

My nerve endings crackle. "Did we? I don't remember saying that." I'm a crap liar. I can barely get the words out because he's standing so close I can feel the heat from his body and his breath on my cheek.

"Big, big plans." His hands slowly slide around my middle and he pulls me back against him.

I shiver with desire, but try to keep things light. "Seriously? I wasn't sure you meant it."

"I meant it alright." He kisses my neck and an explosion of nerves ignite my core. His hand wanders lower. "You taste better than any damn cake," he says, his teeth grazing. "Be. My. Valerie," he groans. "Only mine. *Mon dieu*, I think" — another kiss — "we'd better get out" — another kiss — "of this chalet" — his teeth catch my ear lobe — "before I drag you to my bedroom and devour you," he growls.

If I were a cake, I'd be one of those delicious hot chocolate lava cakes with a gooey melting middle. I don't remember promising to be his *anything*, but right now, he could demand anything, do anything, and I'd say, yes, yes, yes bloody please with marshmallows and sprinkles on top.

17

LEO

Leo

Okay, so it's the cheesiest line ever — *Be my Valerie! Bof!* — but she smells and tastes so divine it makes me both tongue-tied and soft headed. And supremely happy. I'm overflowing with all these unexpected emotions. Like being swept away on a hot tidal wave of lust and icy determination to make her mine. Even though she's English, for crying out loud. The irony is not lost on me. I'm conflicted and confused. I'm also an insensitive shit who doesn't know how to be nice. Because the truth is, I would like to lock her in my bedroom and not let her go anywhere. Not that I'd let her know that of course. No need to scare her off. I know how it sounds — fairly Neanderthal wanting to stake my claim and make her exclusively mine, especially after my monumental fuck up on the chairlift, asking her to distract Josh.

I'm sure my feelings will abate. Maybe today, I'll get Valerie out of my system.

Last night, everything was going so well, only to have her slip from my grasp. It was like being struck by lightning. I finally understand why we French say that falling for someone is *un coup de foudre*. A lightning strike. I went to bed feeling stunned, burned to the core, unable to get Valerie from my mind, unable to sleep, unable to think straight. Imagining my hands and mouth on her soft limbs, between her legs, inside her... I want so much to taste my Valerie. But maybe, if lightning comes in a flash, it may go in one too. What I'm most concerned about is that this feeling, this sickness I've been struck with, may be it is permanent. *Mon dieu!*

I have the strangest urges and thoughts swilling in my brain. I can't help but wonder what it might be like to show someone I'm capable of deeper feelings too. Maybe even romance. Maybe a long term commitment. *Bof!*

I drag Valerie from the chalet, unable to believe my own idiocy — I should just take her to bed! Now! Immediately! Romance? *Non! Jamais!* I've locked feelings like that away my entire life. Even my relationship with my siblings is restrained, and if there is such a thing as love, it is what I feel for Hugo and Amé. There is nothing I wouldn't do for them. Hugo may think I'm being over-protective of Amé, but after what our mother went through at the hands of our father, can he really blame me?

But what I feel for Valerie is different to how I've felt about any other woman. I want to protect her. To guard her like a dragon. I want to breathe fire into her.

This morning, even though she can barely look at me, I think she may not be entirely cold to me. That is good. Don't ask me why that is good, but it seems important she has a better opinion of me. If I am to be her boss, I try to convince myself — some fucking boss! — I should make her see I'm not a totally selfish arsehole. Of course, I totally am.

But my words, *Be my Valerie*, repeating in my head making me cringe. I think I may have overstepped. Lost my head. It was not a good idea to kiss her again. She looked shell-shocked. *Be my Valerie.* What an idiotic thing to say. It's almost like saying, *Be mine. Be my wife.*

This girl makes it impossible for me to keep my cool, but as the French like to say, *Impossible n'est pas Français.* Impossible isn't French.

Once she is out of earshot, having gone to get her coat, I kick the skirting board. "Leo, you dumb fucking ass, try to act as if your brain hasn't been totally fried by lightning."

18

VALERIE

Valerie

The day takes on a dreamlike quality. We walk hand-in-hand back to Jean-Luc's house and I think we're going to go off on the snowmobile again, but instead Jean-Luc is around the back in his yard in the process of hitching six dogs to a sled.

"Oh. Wow!"

Leo is watching me closely. "Go ahead, you can stroke them. The dogs are friendly."

Jean-Luc introduces them. Bashful, Doc, Sleepy, Happy, Dopey and Sneezy. Following his lead, I crouch down to pet them.

"No Grumpy?" I ask.

Jean-Luc cracks a laugh, showing a couple of missing teeth. "With a musher like Leo? Why would you need Grumpy?"

He has a point, though it looks suspiciously like Leo is trying to suppress a grin. He barks something in French and they both start laughing. He strokes the dogs' heads and scratches behind their ears. *Well, hello! I'm over here!* The lucky dogs seem very familiar with Leo, competing for his attention; I tell myself that as much as I'm tempted to do the same, I really must try to maintain some decorum. I listen to the men chatting, wishing I knew what they were saying, and making a resolution there and then to improve my French-speaking skills.

"Jump on board," says Leo.

"You really know how to do this?"

"I'd like to think so. It's been a while, but hopefully we won't end up in a snowdrift."

Again, I wouldn't complain.

The dogs are barking like crazy, ready to set off. I hop aboard and Jean-Luc waves. Leo shouts something, presumably at the dogs not me, gives a snap of the reins and we're off.

If I thought the skidoo snowmobile was fun, this is something else. Maybe it's the rush of air, the swoosh of the sled on ice beneath me, and the sound of the dogs' paws pounding the snow. We fly over bumps and I hold on tighter. I spot a hut in the distance and Leo shouts instructions to the dogs. We slow down and stop right outside the door. I'm guessing it's one of Jean-Luc's shepherd's huts.

Leo unhitches the dogs and ushers me and them inside.

It's a simple one-room building made of stone with a plain wooden table, a couple of wooden chairs, a fireplace and a narrow bed in the corner that I struggle to tear my eyes away from.

Leo has brought lunch (baguettes) and a flask of coffee. He's also brought water and snacks for the dogs. After a bit of snapping, the dogs settle down on the floor together. I chew my baguette and cheese nervously as Leo recounts anecdotes from his childhood. He's funny. Good company. And self-deprecating. Not at all the arrogant misery guts I originally took him to be. He asks me about my own childhood and I'm surprised to find myself opening up, telling him about my mother bringing us kids up single-handed, her heartbreak when my father died.

Leo's dark eyes search mine. "That must be where you get your fighting spirit."

"Me? A fighter? I think you mean Gemma." I can't help but think about what a loser I have been, wasting so much time moping after Simon.

"No. You too. Look how you shimmied up that climbing wall and didn't whine about any of the stag party stuff, even though you clearly didn't want to be there. You're a very good friend to Gemma. And you haven't given up on the skiing yet, have you?"

"I suppose not."

"I think you're full of, how do I put it...? Yorkshire grit."

I laugh. "A Yorkshire monkey full of grit, is that how you'd describe me?"

He takes my hand. "Non, I have a few other adjectives in mind, but I'm not used to giving compliments."

"Ha, well, I'm not exactly used to receiving them either."

"I believe you could have a wonderful cookery business in Yorkshire."

Oh. I feel slightly deflated. I don't want to think about going home.

"You're your own person. You can be whoever you want. You can do whatever you want, Valerie."

Leo coughs and blushes. It's the cutest thing ever.

I stand up and make my way to his side of the table. I sit on his lap, straddling his knees and stare into his dark chocolate eyes. "Well, if I can be who I want," I pull off his hat, "and do what I want," I rake my fingers through his thick locks, "it's this. I've been wanting to do this for a long time."

A slow smile spreads on his lips. "Oh, really, since when?"

I don't answer. Instead, I kiss him. Today feels like a gift. His hands draw me closer, his tongue ignites a hot flame inside me and there's no missing the physical need in him even through all his snow gear.

"Valerie, I want nothing more than to make you mine," he growls, as if the thought pains him.

Unfortunately, I'm not sure if it's Leo's tone of voice that starts it, but one of the dogs growls too. And it seems to set off a chain reaction. Suddenly it's mayhem, a den of barking and growling and Leo shouting. I get off his knee in a hurry, and he opens the door and orders the dogs outside. "*Zut!* We'd better get them back home. They're restless," he says.

The dogs aren't the only ones. I have a raging hunger for Leo, which needs to be satisfied.

Beside the sled, Leo asks if I'd like to take control of the dogs. He explains what to do and we swap over. It's good to have something to concentrate on, and it's not as difficult as it looks. To be honest, the dogs do the hard graft. They seem to know where they're going and what to do. I wish I did.

19

LEO

Leo

I think Valerie and I may be equally desperate to get back to the chalet before anyone else returns. I want to fuck her brains out. Fuck he until she cries for mercy. But fucking Jean-Luc insists on us sharing a glass of wine and some cheese with him before we leave. His conversation rambles and increasingly, frustratingly, Valerie looks enthralled. I shouldn't begrudge the old man her company. After lending us his dogs and sled, and the snowmobile, I can hardly refuse him. But as the shadows lengthen and the daylight slips away, so does our chance of spending time alone together in the chalet, and I'm close to throttling my uncle.

Valerie's and my eyes keep latching on to one anothers as Jean-Luc rambles on about the weather and the tourists and how much the place has changed since he was a boy. Valerie is a good listener. She appears fascinated by every little detail, plying him for more information, laughing at his anecdotes. The old boy is clearly loving her attention, and I don't blame him. Who wouldn't be charmed by her enthusiasm? I have to remind myself not to be impatient with him, nor jealous, seeing her hanging off his every word and throwing her head back with laughter.

But God, I want to kiss the exposed skin of her throat.

Eventually, I manage to make our excuses and drag her away from Jean-Luc's.

My phone rings as we're getting into the car. "It's Amé," I say, and notice I've already missed a previous call from her.

"Aren't you going to answer it?" asks Valerie, looking out of the car window.

"No. I'll see her tomorrow. Right now, all I want to do is this." I take her chin and draw her toward me. I cannot resist kissing Valerie, exploring her body. Maybe a bit possessively. I know I'm being overbearing, but I cannot get enough of her and she's kept me waiting all this time. I am not a patient man. Although I respect Jean-Luc like a father, the last two hours feels like a decade wasted because it's time we could have had alone. And Amé, God love her, can wait too.

Only half joking, I ask Valerie why she kept badgering Jean-Luc with more questions when we could've been out of there hours ago.

"Well, I thought you probably wanted to spend some time with your uncle, and to be honest, it was all fascinating information for what I'm writing." She sounds a bit subdued. She turns her head away from me again and I berate myself. Honestly, I need to calm down and not put pressure on her. Instead, as we set off again, I encourage her to tell me about her writing.

She's writing a novel set in France about a single father and the widow next door; unfortunately, it sounds a lot like my brother's life for real — single father and selfish bitch of an ex-wife, falling in love with his neighbor — but I don't tell her that. No need to burst her bubble.

I park up the car outside the chalet and Valerie touches my arm. "I just want you to know, no matter what happens … with Amé, I had a great time today. Thank you."

That makes me exceedingly happy. "Was it champion?"

"Aye. More than." She leans forwards and kisses me lightly. I close my eyes, ready for more, but she's gone, leaping out of the car and rushing indoors. Left aching with longing, I give chase, but pull up short when I hear the mob upstairs.

Valerie has disappeared into the kitchen. I follow, quietly shutting the door behind me. I put my finger to my lips. Pinning her against the fridge, I kiss her again. "I want you so badly," I groan. "Do you feel it too?" My raging hard-on is difficult to miss pressed up against her, but I want her to know, I hope my kiss conveys, my day has also been a day fit for a champion. As a matter of fact, she has made this whole week a wonderful one instead of the disaster I'd anticipated.

Valerie gently but firmly pushes me away.

"What's the matter?" I ask.

"Nothing," she whispers, looking over my shoulder. "I'm just not..." Her face is troubled. She's not even looking at me.

My breath catches in my throat. She doesn't want this like I do. She doesn't want. Us.

"Gemma must be busy buying something in town," she says. "I'd better get started on tonight's meal or that lot through there'll be grumbling."

Step away, Leo, step away. Mortified, I let my hands fall to my sides. How could I have misjudged the situation so badly? "As long as that's all it is. Do you need any help in here?"

"No. Not at all. You go and chat to the guys. Find out what they've all been up to. Keep them occupied and out of my hair. Go on!" she says, giving me a push toward the door.

The guys have decimated the cake, leaving only crumbs. I pour myself a glass of wine and sit down. For a while I listen to their banter, before I realize one of them is missing.

"Where's Josh?" I ask.

They look around the room as if they've only just realized that the groom is not among them. None of them know.

"And where's Gemma?"

"Come to think of it, I haven't seen either of them since lunchtime," says Antoine stretching.

"Didn't Gemma have a problem with her ski?" asks Harry.

"Oh yeah, she went to replace her ski, that's right, and Josh went with her. Haven't heard hide nor hair from either of them since," says Benoit, getting up and pouring himself another drink.

"Me neither," adds Guillame.

"*Putain*!" I explode. I am so ready to hit something. Someone. "None of you have seen Josh or Gemma all afternoon? Weren't you worried about that?"

A hundred questions run through my brain. I ring Josh's phone. There's no answer. The same goes for Gemma. Something is not right. It makes me fucking uneasy. "What if there's been an accident? Didn't any of you think to check?"

"I'm sure they'll be fine," says Antoine, scratching his stomach.

"No, we need to find out where they are. First we check they're not here. Shit, I'll do it myself," I say when none of them seem in a hurry to get up. "Which room was Josh in?"

'With me," says Harry. "Top of the stairs, first room on the right."

Not caring that they are looking at me as if I'm being a drama queen, I dash upstairs, taking them two at a time. Something feels wrong about this. Alarm bells are ringing. I throw open the door to the bedroom and my heart sinks as I look around. Josh isn't trapped on the mountain and there hasn't been a dreadful accident: if I'm not mistaken, there's only one suitcase in here. I check the cupboards and the bathroom, just to be sure.

Then I run down two flights of stairs to check Gemma's room.

Valerie is standing outside the door with a letter in her shaking hands. Her face is as white as the sheet of paper.

"I don't believe it. She's gone. Gemma's flipping gone off with Josh."

20

VALERIE

Last night I didn't sleep a wink. Having read the awful letter from Gemma, knowing that the shit was about to hit the fan, I'd stood outside our bedrooms for ages trying to work up the courage to go and find Leo.

Instead, he found me.

"Is this why you were in no fucking hurry to get back here? You were in on their little plan to run away together? Buying them more time," he snarls, his eyes bright with fury.

"God, no. I had no idea."

"*Bof*! And yet you and Gemma are such close friends."

From the look of things, he's spitting angry, fighting to keep his temper under control. I understand he's upset, but damn it, so am I!

"Why are you blaming this on me? Gemma and I don't tell each other every little thing. It's got nothing to do with me!"

"It has *everything* to do with you. You are always covering for her." He snatches the letter from my hands.

"That's not true."

"Be honest for once. *Merde*! You women! I cannot believe this! When were you going to tell me? Amé is coming tomorrow to pick up Josh! To surprise him. She's going to be fucking devastated."

"Well, maybe you should've thought of that before you started trying to fuck up her relationship with Josh. I'd have thought this would make you happy."

He glares at me. "Happy? What on earth are you talking about? Why would Amé being upset make me happy? All I ever wanted was her happiness."

I gulp. "Oh, really. That wasn't the impression I got when you asked me to...you know, on the chairlift... You don't give a damn as long as Amé chooses the right man!"

"Yes ... the right man." He runs a hand through his hair, distracted.

"Well done," I say clapping my hands. "Now you're in the clear, aren't you? This is exactly what you planned all along."

"I did not plan this. I know I suggested ... for a while it was true, I thought it might be best if she didn't marry Josh. Look, I cocked up, but this is not how I wanted things to turn out."

"Isn't it? Don't bother pretending to be so outraged, Leo, it's what you planned! Now you can be there to comfort her, to be her shoulder to cry on. How convenient! You now have Amé all for yourself!"

I push past him and run upstairs. Leo follows. I try to slam shut the kitchen door, but he barges it open.

"Are you crazy? Have you totally lost your little mind? What are you talking about?" he demands.

"Don't call me crazy! You're the one with the bloody mad scheming plots!" We glare at one another across the kitchen island. "Why else would you ask me to have some so-called 'fun' with Josh? Today was a bit of a waste of bloody time on both our parts, wasn't it?" I hiss.

He closes his eyes and scrunches up his face in fury. "Maybe it was. But you were deliberately time-wasting! Fuck this shit!" He slaps the letter in his hand on the kitchen counter.

Antoine and Benoit open the serving hatch. "Everything okay in here? You alright, Valerie, darling?"

The color leeches from Leo's face. It's as if he'd seen a ghost. He swallows and clenches his fists at his sides. "I'm sorry you feel like you do. *Merde*, I'm sorry you *think* like you do. I'm sorry you ever came here. Excuse me, I need to call Amé." He stalks out.

"Go ahead!" I shout after him, my chest heaving with sobs. "I need to cook supper for *your* bloody guests anyway! No offence, Antoine, Benoit."

"None taken, Valerie."

"Can you fuck off and leave me to cook then!" I snarl.

Everyone melts away, and I close the serving hatch. Damn! Shaking, I lean on the kitchen counter trying to catch my breath, but no matter how how much I curse at myself the stupid tears keep leeching from my eyes.

I cannot believe I forgot all this crazy stuff about Leo and Amé. I cannot believe I let myself fall for him. Talk about out of the frying pan and into the fire. I'm not the crazy one, he is. What a meddling bastard! Trying to destroy his friend's relationship, while all the time behind his back he's been scheming. Why bother pretending to be so upset about Josh going off with Gemma? Why bother pretending he's into me when he's clearly in love with Amé? If the bastard even knows what love is. Another sob escapes me.

I slam a few cupboard doors. No more men in my life. Never! Except, of course, I have to cook seven of the bastards' supper tonight. Where the hell is the arsenic in this pantry? And what the bloody hell am I going to cook? I'm seriously all out of ideas.

Right then, of all the times he could have chosen, my phone pings with a text from Simon.

> Hey Val, I think I may have made a horrible mistake. I was thinking I could maybe visit you in Méricoeur. Miss you so much! x

A bark of insane laughter escapes me. It's all I'd wanted a few days ago, but now I hurriedly text my response:

> No thanks, Simon! Too late. Not missing you at all, so sod off and leave me alone!

I think I may have heartburn. Or maybe I'm having a seizure. I have a pain in my chest like a gaping wound, but I have to keep going. If I stop, I might never get back on my feet. I think of Gemma's words on the phone all those weeks ago when I made the decision to come here. It's a shock, it's humiliating, but I need to keep skiing. *I can ski*, I tell myself. *I may look like an ugly duckling, but I can ski.*

Next door, while I'm boiling potatoes and trying to let off my head of steam, I half listen to Leo interrogating the guys some more. How long has the relationship between Gemma and Josh been going on? What did they notice? When? Why didn't they say anything? They don't seem any wiser than me, the poor sods.

Then Leo opens the kitchen hatch and sticks his head through the opening.

"Have you called Gemma yet?" he asks.

I'd like to slam those doors in his face. We glare at each other. But shit, I haven't called her, and I should have. "Yes. I. Have!" I lie. "I left a message, but she didn't pick up." I turn my back on him, so he can't see the tears which have sprung to my eyes.

I slap the saucepan of potatoes on the dining table with a pack of butter. "You're going to have to look after yourselves tonight, lads. Sorry. I'm feeling unwell." I rush downstairs and call Gemma.

"Gemma, you stupid cow. Where the bloody hell are you, and what do you think you're doing running off with—?"

Halfway through my voice message, she rings me. "Valerie. I'm so, so sorry. Believe me, I couldn't be sorrier. I know I've been a terrible friend keeping you in the dark!" She sounds choked. But not as choked as she's going to sound when I'm through strangling her.

She explains the whole situation. She and Josh have fallen hopelessly in love. He called Amé this morning to tell her that he had to call the wedding off. She was understandably upset and said Leo would probably murder them both, so he and Gemma thought it might be prudent if they both moved out of her brother's chalet and into a hotel before that occurred.

"Wait, what?" Goosebumps spread up my arms. "What do you mean her brother's chalet?"

"Leo's," says Gemma.

"But you said Amé's brother."

"Yes, dumbass. Leo is Amé's brother."

"Oh God. I thought he was in love with her. I thought … I said all those horrible things…" I slide down the wall to the floor.

"Valerie, are you still there? You know I was joking, right? I mean Amé is Leo's brother, but you're not a dumbass, I am. But this is the real deal, Val. I love Josh. You of all people should understand that. You write about love for goodness sake. This is like nothing I've ever felt before. It's like we're made for one another…"

What a bloody mess. It still doesn't make what Leo asked me to do right, but it makes it more understandable. And I am a bloody dumbass. And she's not the only one hopelessly in love.

21

LEO

Leo

Early the next morning, I drive the guys to the airport and to be honest, it's a relief to see them go. I'm worn out and in no mood for conversation. I have been on the phone with either Amé or Hugo most of the night. She is going to stay with Hugo for a while. He could do with some help with the kids and it will take her mind off things.

When I get back to the chalet, the first thing I do is seek out Valerie. She is packing her bags. Oh God, where do I even begin? How do I patch things up?

"What are you doing?" I ask.

"Leaving," she says.

My throat tightens.

"I imagine you want me out of here. Probably permanently. Excuse me, I need to get my toiletries."

I inhale her own sweet nectar, her home-baked flowery scent as she brushes past me and goes into the bathroom. She returns with her toiletry bag and I get another lungful making me feel lost already. I am lost for words. I feel sick. How is it I could have so comprehensively messed up not only my sister's relationship, but my own chances of something special as well? Not that there was a relationship with Valerie, but perhaps, if I'd been a little more careful, a little less inconsiderate and fucking selfish, there could have been.

"I know you didn't know about Gemma and Josh. I was wrong to accuse you of being involved. And so very wrong to ask you to distract Josh—"

"—to do anything with Josh!" she snaps.

"Yes. Agreed. I regret asking. And I'm sorry for saying what I did last night. I told you I make mistakes." But it doesn't sound genuine. I sound wooden and I can't seem to let go of the anger. I don't want to feel anything for Valerie. But I do. And now she is walking out on me. I want to be the person I was before I met her. Detached from my emotions. Safe in my working bubble. But it's as if she's come along with a hammer and cracked me wide open.

"I'm genuinely sorry for Amé," she says. "I had no idea she's your sister. I thought … it doesn't matter what I thought."

It does matter. It doesn't make her sorry enough to stop folding her clothes and placing them in her suitcase.

"You're going to leave, just like that? Permanently?"

She glances my way. "I think this is for the best, don't you? And you've got a full week to find another chalet host. I'm sure they're a dime a dozen. I shouldn't be hard to replace."

She is ridiculous. And impossible to replace. "No, I'm sure that'll be no problem."

She winces, and it makes me feel better. For about two seconds.

She zips up her bag and gets out her phone. And then she looks at me. "So, what's the telephone number for a taxi in France? As you seem to be a walking telephone directory, perhaps you would be kind enough to share. Before we go our separate ways." She bites her lip. Silent tears spill from her eyes and trail down her cheeks as she looks at her phone. She might as well have stuck a knife in my heart. She gives herself a shake and puts a hand up to stop me coming closer. "Sorry! I'm just—"

I pull her into my arms, crushing her against me. "God, Valerie.

No, I'm sorry. I'm so sorry, I've been such a thoughtless, selfish, arrogant pig. I was trying to sort everything out for Amé, and I wanted to get everyone out of the chalet so we could be together and I could talk to you in private, but then when I got back here, and you were packing your bags... I don't want that. Don't go! I know I'm a horrible person. I am an arrogant shit ... to be honest, I'm appalled by myself. I'm not making excuses, but I wanted the best for Amé. And I didn't want to admit I had developed feelings for you..."

"You have been pretty horrible." Valerie sniffs. "I really had no idea about Gemma." She's limp in my arms, still holding on to her bag. "What sort of feelings hav you developed for me?" She asks in a small voice.

Here goes. I'd better think hard before I open my fat mouth. I stroke her hair behind her ear. "I feel like a French idiot. An overbearing fool who ... who doesn't want you to go anywhere. My actions are impossible to explain without sounding like a monster. Like my father." That realization cuts to the bone. I feel so ashamed, I extricate myself and turn my back on her. "My father could be cruel, and though perhaps it's true, I am like him, a little, I would never hurt you. He hurt our mother badly. The very thought of anyone touching you makes me sick. That's why it is so important that Amé finds the right sort of man. A man who will look after her and keep her happy. Cherish her. I would really like, very much, for you not to think of me as a complete monster."

Her arms thread through mine around my waist and she presses her face against my back, hugging me tightly. "You're not a monster, Leo. Far from it. I understand why you did what you did, even though I think perhaps you could have found a better way ... Where Amé is concerned, your heart is in the right place, even if your words weren't."

I turn around and stare down at her. I want to cup her precious face between my palms, but I'm too scared even to touch her and risk breaking this fragile truce. "Can you forgive me? For asking you to seduce Josh? I must have been out of my mind!"

There's a pause. "I forgave that days ago. I'm the one who's sorry.

For doubting you. For not giving you the chance to explain about Amé in full."

"I should never have put you in that position. Even the thought that I asked you to be some sort of distraction to Josh ... before I developed such strong feelings ... now it makes me feel ..." A shudder overwhelms me.

Pulling my clenched fists to her lips, Valerie kisses my knuckles. "You were saying ... Can we go back to your feelings? So how strong are these feelings? I think you could elaborate."

Mon Dieu. I may not be my father, but I am still a bad man. I can no longer think of Amé and all her woes, all that fills my head is Valerie.

"I feel like you should leave me before I crush you in my arms. I am not good enough for you ... But if you go, I will ... I think will be destroyed. I am undeserving of your attention or affection or...or—"

"—or love?"

I smile and wipe away the vestiges of her tears with my thumbs. "Or love. I am certainly undeserving of your love."

"I feel you could express this so much better in your bedroom," she says.

I cannot help but smile. "There is a lot more space there than in this cramped little room. The bed is much larger than this tiny one and and I have big feelings!"

She sighs. "Just big feelings? I thought your English was so much better than that..." She gazes up at me coquettishly and my heart seizes.

"I have been waiting too long to show you my big—"

She puts a finger over my lips.

I continue talking. "When you are with me, I am lost for words, but also I feel *champion.*"

"Now you're talking!" She grins, jumps up and wraps her legs around my hips. "Boy, you certainly know how to flatter a girl." She kisses me and my cock is on immediate alert. "If you really want me to stay," she says between kisses, "I may need some further persuading ... some convincing...Oh, I think I feel some evidence after all."

She smiles lasciviously and I carry her toward the stairs.

"Like I said, *big* feelings. Could I persuade you to take this conversation upstairs?"

"Oh, it looks like you're already en route. If you say nice things to me in your sexiest French accent, I might not notice that you have taken my agreement for granted."

"*Ah, mon petit diable, mon caneton, mon singe, mon coeur,*" I growl, not at all sure I'll make it to my bedroom...

EPILOGUE

Valerie

Summer in the French Alps is green and glorious. It is not always as conducive to my writing as I'd like because Leo has a tendency to interrupt my train of thought and he is not an easy man to resist and he's a spectacular distraction.

One particularly sunny day not long ago, when the sky was a lustrous shade of blue, Leo and I went for a mountain hike. It's a bit of trek up to our favorite trail to the shepherd's hut carrying all our gear on our backs. Well, to be honest, Leo carries most of it.

Half way there, Leo leads me away from the track to a secluded meadow. He lays a blanket on the grass and says we are stopping for a picnic. I don't complain. The view is breathtaking, magnificent — *champion!* — and that's just Leo mind: the mountains and valley are pretty eye-catching too. We eat our baguettes and, as is often the case with Leo, he seems to get an idea in his head halfway through eating. He runs a hand down my bare thigh and I look his way.

Instead of lunch, it's me he has an appetite for. Alfresco.

He feeds me a grape and smiles as I chew. Playing dumb, I lie back on the grass and close my eyes. A soft breeze curls around my limbs and he tucks a tendril of loose hair behind my ear.

"You're so damn beautiful," whispers Leo.

"In French," I say.

Even with my eyes closed, I can almost sense him smiling. Talking French nonsense, he kisses my eyelids and the tip of my nose. A casual hand undoes the button and zip of my shorts. "Gardez les yeux fermés" he whispers. *Keep your eyes closed.* His hand slides beneath the waistband of my shorts, beneath the elastic of my underwear, between my legs. I am so ready for him.

"Kiss me. Make love to me," I say.

"Not yet. I'm too busy ... sightseeing."

He chuckles as I moan with pleasure. Hot lights flash behind my eyelids as my desire swells. Heat rushes from his fingertips to my core spreading throughout my body. "I want to taste... you!" I gasp, arching as he strokes me ever nearer to a crescendo.

"Not yet. I have an appetite for you and you know how selfish I can be." His tongue accompanies his fingers. He licks lovingly and grazes teasingly and thrusts deep into my core; I whimper and writhe in response lost to the exquisite pressure.

"Oh, my God, Leo! Leo!" Whoever knew lovemaking could be like this? Whoever knew the body was capable of soaring? I gasp as his low rumble of laughter reverberates through me. "Hush, *mon petit diable.*"

This is no laughing matter. Sound and sensation combine, nerve endings stretch, fireworks flash behind my eyelids. My eyes fly open and I cry out as the coil of tension in me snaps unleashing an orgasm like an avalanche that floods through me and over me and out of me. I close my eyes again to dazzling bioluminescence over a deep, blue ocean.

He kisses me then. "You opened your eyes."

I laugh. "Impossible not to." I blink at the brightness of the sun and his deep brown eyes and smiling face hovering above me. "I love you," I say, unabashedly.

"Je t'adore," he replies.

We continue to make *slow, leisurely love* beneath the expansive blue canopy of sky, caressed by the fresh mountain air. *Slow* because after my shattering orgasm I'm in no condition to rush. *Leisurely* because I want to take my time appreciating every milimeter of the miracle that is Leo. *Love* because, I imagine, if he feels halfway close to how I feel, there is no other word to describe this. This union is love. I want to shout my love to the mountains. When I come again, I do.

Afterwards we lie sated and smiling in that smug way lovers have, holding hands, staring at a couple of clouds drifting overhead, watching a bird of prey wheeling high above, listening to the hum of my blood and to nature all around us.

I fall asleep with the sun warming my face and Leo warming my heart. I cannot imagine life gets any better than this.

Some time later, I suggest we really should resume our hike; Leo groans and it's not me who's struggling to get up off the ground. Fair enough, I think, maybe he has cramp after our uphill hike, or maybe all that love-making has worn him out, or most likely he's expended rather a lot of more additional energy than me since we supposedly sat down for lunch. Rather guiltily, I acknowledge the latter is probably true. He may think of himself as selfish, but he's a selfless lover.

I grab his hand and trying to be of assistance, attempting to haul him to his feet.

"No. Wait," he snaps.

For a moment, I'm taken aback. Then gripped by concern. Is he alright? Is he in pain? I step forward—

"Non! Arrêt! Patience!"

"Says the most patient man ever." I roll my eyes.

What's he doing down there on one knee, fumbling in his pockets? Is he having some sort of seizure?

And then he holds up a small blue jewelry box. He opens it and a diamond sparkles in the sunlight. He looks up at me, his gaze hot, his cheeks flushed, his beautiful eyes shining. "I have been trying to ask you something for a few days now, but I could never find the right moment or place," he says. "Will you marry me, Valerie? *Tu es tout pour moi.*" You are my everything.

Trembling, with tears in my eyes, I nod. "Yes. Oh, yes, Leo!"

Beaming, he slides the ring on my finger.

I clasp his face and kiss him tenderly. *"Tu es tout pour moi. Pour toujours!"* I say in my terrible French accent, and it's the truth. Leo is my everything. Forever.

The End

Thank you so much for reading Valerie and Leo's story. I hope you had as much fun reading about their romantic journey, as I had writing it. If you enjoyed it, please spread the word, and if you'd like to read another of my romance novellas, don't wait. Grab it here!

If you'd like to support me and find out about what's in the pipeline, I'd be thrilled if you joined my newsletter. Sign up for it by clicking here: Anna's Foxtrot

ALSO BY ANNA FOXKIRK

Passport to Love series

Holly Ever After

The Worst Noelle

Be My Valerie

Alice in Wanderlust

❄

Want to read a snippet of *The Worst Noelle?*

Imagine one wealthy American society snob and throw her in a hot world of trouble...

Chapter One

The novelty of slumming it wears off after about ten minutes of traveling economy. There's no elbow space. There's no leg space. There's not even space for my Balenciaga handbag. I call over the air stewardess.

"These seats have limited reclining because they're in front of the lavatories," she explains with a pinched expression on her face.

"No, really. You call this limited?" I mutter.

"There was the option to select your seat when you booked your flight, madam." She annunciates every word as if I am an idiot.

We lock eyes and I smile though I would like to strangle her with her natty nylon neck scarf. It's enough to make me break out in hives.

By the time I'd got round to booking my flights there hadn't exactly been many seat options left, and besides, after drowning my woes in a bottle of Beaujolais, I'd been in no fit state to make carefully considered decisions. After retrieving the wedding invitation from the trash, I'd impulsively bought my tickets and only then rung Lara in New Zealand to let her know the good news. "Hey, Lara! It's me!"

"Noelle?" she'd groaned. "What time is it?"

I took another gulp of my wine, valiantly fighting off the first pincer grip of hangover. "Sorry, did I wake you babe?"

"Mmm. Don't worry. What is it? Is something wrong?"

Don't even get me started. Everything is wrong, the life I have fought so damn hard to build unravelling faster than toilet paper. "No, I have great news! It couldn't wait. I had to let you know, I've changed my mind. There's no way I'm going to miss your wedding. I just booked my flight to New Zealand!"

There's a howling silence. For a moment I think I've lost the connection. "Lara? Lara? Are you still there?"

"Sorry. Did I hear that right? You're coming to New Zealand after all?"

"Yes! That's what I just said. Why? Would you rather I wasn't?"

"No! Of course, not, silly. I'm just a little surprised, is all." I hear shuffling and someone grumbling in the background. Probably her fiancé. I can't believe I haven't even met the guy. I can't believe she's getting married before me.

"I thought you said it was too far to come and you're crazy busy at work right now." When am I ever not crazy busy at work? "And, you have to spend Christmas with your family like always."

Of all the lame excuses. Of course, I could be flying home to the Hamptons right now, wallowing in Foley festive luxury — but, that always comes with a generous side-helping of toxic family bickering. Instead, because of my impulsive and what my dad calls my bone-headed attitude, here I am being spat through the air like a cat's hairball on route to my best friend's wedding. A best friend I haven't seen for over five years and rarely speak to these days.

Besides, that conversation had been over a month ago. A lot can happen in a month. "I was always planning on coming," I lie. "I just had to figure out the details."

"I wasn't expecting it, but that's awesome news! I can't wait to see you, Noelle!"

I hear more mumbling in the background, then Lara whispering, telling someone to go back to sleep.

It had only been the next day, in the sour light of morning, with a vicious hangover for company, as I tried to unpick the previous night's drinking spree and decidedly flighty decisions, that I wondered if I hadn't screwed up. Again. Had Lara sounded a mite unenthusiastic about my impending visit and us rekindling our bestie status? Maybe I should've called her first to check she still wanted me to come. Maybe she would've preferred a generous wedding gift, rather than a heroic gesture—something decadent from her wedding gift list, like an electric sheepshearing handpiece...

Or, maybe not.

Let's be honest, I haven't seen Lara in five years and, if a lot can happen in a month, imagine how much can change in five years. It's somewhat concerning, but too late to rectify.

I am now on a flight bound for New Zealand, the land of the long white cloud. That doesn't sound to me like the most promising sort of holiday or very good marketing. Who needs any more clouds in their life, especially not super long ones? If this is not true loyalty and dedication to our enduring friendship, I don't know what is.

"Any chance of a drink any time soon?" I ask the air stewardess. I know I shouldn't have but flying always makes me nervous as hell. "After such a long delay, we should be entitled to some compensation, don't you think? Like a glass of champagne, perhaps? Sometime in this time zone?"

The air stewardess pouts a pair of botoxed lips. "I'm sorry, ma'am, but there will be no drinks served until after the fasten-your-seatbelt signs have been switched off. You do realize that drinks are not free in this section of the plane?"

Do I look like I can't pay? Who does she think she is?

"Of course, I realize!" As if I need reminding. We will probably have to pay for toilet paper just to wipe our asses. "I don't need reminding, but it would be nice to get little service around here!"

The air stewardess sashays off along the aisle.

"Excuse me? I haven't finished ... Oh, for crying out loud! Just get me a gun already!" It's not exactly an auspicious start to my escape abroad. "Someone put me out of my misery."

Neither of my traveling companions react. I am squished between a rock and a hard place ... actually, more like a rock and a mushroom. Man Mountain in the window seat, ever since giving me a rigorous double take — because clearly women wearing Armani suits are seldom seen in cattle class — has his eyes fixed on a book in his lap, studiously ignoring me. Man Mushroom on my left has already fallen asleep, mouth gaping wide enough to stow a carry-on suitcase.

I cannot help but sigh. "You know how they call these flights *long haul* ... the only way to endure such prolonged torture is steeped in alcohol." Why hadn't I paid for Business Class? I had enough money saved. What warped part of my brain had informed me this would be a wonderful idea? A cocktail-induced coma could have made better choices than me.

"Good book?" I lean toward the Rock in the window seat.

"Mmmhmm." Above his spectacles, his brow knits. I have to be honest, he has it worse than either Mushroom Man or me. Rock's denim-clad knees are mashed hard up against the seat in front. If I wasn't locked in a silent battle for elbow space with him, I might (almost) feel sorry for him, but he lost my vote of sympathy the moment he stole the armrest.

I guess chivalrous behavior doesn't extend beyond Business Class.

Traveling economy is the sort of remedial torture Lara would approve of. From what I can gather, she's become terrifyingly virtuous, practically a saint, having given everything up everything to be with the man she loves. Shaun. Shaun, ugh! The name conjures up sheep shearing and gum boots. The truth is Lara getting married seemed to pour oil onto the fire of my already messed up, usually highly business-focused, brain. I panic-bought those plane tickets, and as we all know, panic-shopping is never a good idea. Nothing like the benefit of hindsight...but unless there's an eject button it's a little too late to extract myself.

A sigh shudders through me. "You'd think after the waiting and all, they'd have provided us with a beverage." I pull out the inflight magazine and with my elbows tucked into my sides like chicken wings, I flick through the pages pretending to be enthralled —Who even buys this crap? It's so overpriced. Meanwhile, the harrowing realization I'm stuck on this plane getting farther and farther away from civilization and closer and closer to what is most likely to be ... the worst wedding, the worst Christmas, the worst mistake ever is beginning to make me feel nauseous.

I reach for the paper barf bag. "Don't worry. I'll be fine," I say to no-one in particular.

Don't get me wrong. I still love Lara despite our losing touch. We have history together. At school we'd been like magnets, practically attached at the hip, living in one another's pockets ... but also, if I'm being totally honest, we also sometimes repelled one another. We grew up in the Pacific Palisades, went to the same private school, liked the same music, but our tastes in pretty much everything could not have been more diametrically opposed. One of the bonuses of that was we never clashed over potential boyfriends or any aspirations for the future. Well, Lara didn't really have aspirations. I was the one with the big dreams.

Once we'd left the closeted existence of high school, Lara and I had gone our separate ways: I'd thrown myself into university and a career, and Lara threw herself into the void — she wanted to see the world. It makes me cringe thinking about some of the whacky and wild stuff she's done over the years from being blessed on one of the floating villages of Lake Titicaca to learning to pole dance in Beijing. I kid you not. That is where she'd met Shaun. Lara used to send me postcards...until one day I received one saying she had found 'the one and only', her 'true love' and decided to stay in New Zealand.

That had come as something of a shock. For two years we didn't write or speak at all. Then the wedding invitation had arrived along with a photo of her and Shaun and a letter asking me to be her maid-of-honor. It had about as much appeal as swallowing the worm in the tequila.

Talking of which, where the heck is my drink? I shove the magazine and barf bag back where they should be. Only twelve more hours to endure ...

On my left, Man Mushroom lets rip with a beer-bellied snore and one of his shirt buttons pops off and hits the chair in front.

"Are you kidding?!" I mutter.

Leg room is not an issue for Mushroom Man. In the airport lounge, at opposite ends of the bar, we'd pretty much matched one another round for round of drinks. When he'd hopped off his barstool to board the plane, I couldn't help but notice he was almost as wide as he was short, and I couldn't have cared less about that … until I found I was seated next to him. The fact he's now infringing on my already limited space, especially if he's going to snore the entire way to Christchurch, is fast becoming a significant issue. Mostly, I resent the fact that the alcohol we'd both consumed in the bar isn't having quite the same anaesthetic effects on me as it evidently is on him.

And his brand of snoring is like being run through with a hacksaw.

I rifle through the pocket of the seat in front of me again. "Did you get any earphones? I don't have any earphones. Did I miss out on that handout?"

Rock's eyes flicker in my direction. In response he huffs and splays his knees wider. He may be tall, but…

"Excuse me. Could you just…?" I corkscrew toward him with my knees, but the look he gives me would crack ice. Seriously? His knee doesn't budge and his face has as much sympathy as a … cliff.

"Do you mind?" he asks and cracks a cheeky-assed grin.

"Yeah, I do mind, actually!" More than he could possibly imagine. It's a tough call not to feel sorry for myself, stuck between the Hacksaw and the Rock, twisted like a goddamn contortionist trying to fit myself into a shoebox with nothing better to do for the next god-damn-how-many hours than mull over the sinkhole of my life. Talk about adding torment to torture. "I know this isn't easy for you, being tall and all, but strictly speaking your knee is encroaching on my space. See here. This is where your space ends." I draw a line in the air from the edge of my seat to his splayed knee. I give his kneecap a poke with my fingernail.

Rock sighs, exasperation tattooed all over his face. "What do you expect me to do about it?"

"Go and sit elsewhere?" I suggest.

His expression does little to ease the hive of frustration building beneath my skin. So what? He's not impressed, but neither am I, and, unfortunately for him, he's making my unbearable situation worse.

His lips compress into a thin line. His knees do not budge even one millimeter. I increase the pressure of my knee against his like it's some sort of competition.

I press the Call button for the air hostess again. And again. And again.

"Careful, you might break a fingernail," says the Rock.

Wow. Is that his idea of pleasant? "I might break more than that," I snap temporarily forgetting the knee competition. He gains a centimeter.

His eyes are focused on whatever his reading, but his lips twitch.

"I don't think my call button works. Could I try yours?" Without waiting for an answer, I reach over and press his call button.

"Talking of encroaching on space…you sure you wouldn't like to put your feet up while you're at it. Perhaps you'd like a foot massage." He doesn't smile.

"I would actually, but not from the likes of you."

"No-one's going to come. As the lady said, you have to wait until the fasten-your-seatbelt lights have been extinguished."

"Yes, but like *I* said, if I don't get a drink or a little more *leg room*, I'm going to be doing some extinguishing of my own. This is the worst flight. The worst everything!"

As if listening, the plane gives a shudder.

"Woah! What the hell was that?"

"Ladies and gentlemen, please remain seated with your seatbelts fastened. We're anticipating flying into some turbulence," says the pilot over the speakers.

"Perfect. How many more hours of this do they expect us to endure? No, don't tell me, I don't want to know." I scrabble around in my handbag beneath the seat muttering to myself. "Should've flown Business Class. This is what comes of making impulsive decisions. Never again!" Pushing my hair out of my face, I brandish a bottle of champagne. "Ha! Never fear. This calls for duty free." Even though I'd bought it to give to Lara. She'll understand an emergency of this nature. "Would you be so kind as to pop the cork? Oh, darn, we don't have glasses. What the hell, I'm traveling economy, it wouldn't be inappropriate to drink straight of the bottle. Would it?"

Rock looks at me as if I have grown two heads. He makes no move to take the bottle from my hand.

"I'm not contaminated, if that's what you're worried about. Anyway, if I were it's too late for you anyway. Couldn't get much closer. Any chance of a hand opening this? I'll share."

"No thank you ... *Princess*," he mutters.

My mouth drops open. Did my ears just deceive me? "Did you just call me a Princess? You...you...uhhh! How rude!" I glare at him, then stuff my bottle back in my bag.

He's got his eyes glued to his book, but a goddamn irritating smile dances about his lips.

From his accent, I've gathered he's clearly a New Zealander ... or at any rate most definitely Neanderthal. To be honest, I can never quite distinguish between the Australian and New Zealand accent. Wherever he's from, he's damn rude. "What gives you the right to call someone you don't even know a princess?"

Our eyes clash again. I have to admit, his are actually somewhat arresting. Pale gray, ringed with black. "Put it this way, from the way you've been fidgeting for the last hour and that bottle of Cristal, not to mention all the bellyaching you've been doing, I don't get the impression you're used to roughing it, darl. Not at all. A prime example of the pea and the princess."

I suck in a breath. I'm actually weirdly kind of flattered which confuses me, but I know how to look affronted. I arch an eyebrow. "You know what, an apology would be nice."

"I agree," he says.

"S-s-sorry?" I splutter.

"Apology accepted. Now if you don't mind"— He lifts his book— "this is interesting." And he resumes reading.

"That was *not* an apology from me. *You* are the one who should be apologizing."

I am ignored.

His open disregard for me is disconcerting. It's another alarming sign that I'm losing my grip.

Up until three months ago, I felt invincible — on top of the world, on top of my job, on top of my man— Cole. Now my life is a dungheap and the crap is piled so high on top of me I can't breathe. I am literally suffocating. Like it's a truly good-for-nothing day when someone as ordinary as the Rock is immune to my feminine charms. It doesn't take a mind-reader to see he a) doesn't find me remotely attractive b) disapproves c) is not a gentleman d) is not the slightest bit interested in my welfare, and e) wishes he'd chosen to sit anywhere else other than next to the highly-strung wreckage taking up space in 49 B.

"I am not a princess!" I whine. Far from it. I have had to make sacrifices to get to the top. I'm beginning to worry if those sacrifices were not worth it. I groan as I rifle through the contents of my handbag. The only remedy come up with is some Rose Hibiscus Face Mist. "Well, this flight is going to be a joy, isn't it?" I say spritzing liberally. "Are all New Zealanders like you?"

"Like what?"

I show him my perfect teeth. They are worth every cent. "Like totally lacking in manners of sensitivity."

The bastard smiles. He also has perfect teeth. "Shit, yeah."

"Look, clearly this is not an ideal situation...but if we're going to be stuck cheek to jowl, we could at least try to be civil to one another, don't you think?" I say, magicking some diplomatic charm from somewhere.

"Does that involve being spritzed?"

"You're hilarious." I purse my lips and put my spritzer away. "I'm Noelle. Noelle Foley." I offer my hand. "And you are ...?"

"Sam Devine."

I laugh. Perhaps a little too hard. "*Divine*. You're kidding! That's your surname? For real?"

"D.*E*.V.I.N.E," he spells out, stressing the e.

"So, Mr *De*-vine. What do you do when you're not being a—"

The plane suddenly drops two feet.

"—*jeeeeerk!*" My stomach hits my throat. We lurch upwards again and another yelp escapes me. I brace myself against the seat in front. The growl of the engines has increased to a deafening roar.

"Perhaps the issues they were having before we took off didn't get fixed," he says.

"Oh, gee, thanks for that reassurance!"

"Please remain seated and ensure your seatbelts are fastened," intones the pilot.

"Like we're going anywhere!" I mutter.

The plane drops again—it could be five feet, it could be fifty.

"Arrrrggg!" I yelp and grab hold of the armrests only to realize my nails are digging into flesh and bone. Sam's arm. I should remove my hand, I know I should, but right now the plane is shaking us around like it's trying to make cocktails.

"Oh, no, this is not....Oh hell!" I whimper.

We're buffeted and tossed. The engine whine rises to a crescendo.

I squeeze my eyes closed. I'm not letting go of Sam Devine any time soon. "Distract me. Talk to me. Say something. De-*vine!*" The last syllable is a shriek as we plummet once more.

"Do you have a phobia of flying by any chance?" Sam's voice is ridiculously calm.

"No! Just a phobia of dying!"

"There is a one in three point three billion chance of dying in a commercial airplane crash and over ninety-eight per cent of plane crashes don't result in fatality," says Sam.

"Terrific! How's that meant to make me feel any better? What are you, an actuary? Oh, for the love of—!"

"What's happening?" Even Man Mushroom has risen from the dead.

"Just some turbulence. We'll be fine," says Sam, casual as you like.

"You don't know that! This isn't just ordinary turbulence! I am not fine!" I screech as my stomach careens as we drop downward again. "I can't stand this. I can't. Why did I think going to New Zealand for my best friend's wedding was a great idea? I must have been out of my mind. I am so sorry. Whatever I did to deserve this, I'm so, so sorry. If you're listening God..."

"Take a few deep breaths. We seem to be through the worst of it," says Sam.

I gulp, but can't seem to get enough air in my lungs.

"Seriously. It's alright. It's easing up."

I open one eye. He could be right. The jumping around seems to have petered out and the engines have settled into a steady rhythm again.

"You can let go of me now," says Sam.

I look at his forearm — "Oh. Sorry!" — and unhook my nails. I've dug white crescents into his skin.

"Could be worse," he says, rubbing his forearm.

"Yes, we could have died. You two could be the last two people I ever talked to. That was crazy. I need a drink more than ever. Right now. Seatbelt signs on or not." I press the call button again. "How come you're so damn calm?"

He pushes his reading glasses up his nose. "Well, I have to deal with some fairly challenging situations in my line of work."

"I thought you were an actuary," I say.

He goes back to reading his book.

"No, go on. Tell me. What do you do for a living?"

"Nothing that would interest you." He doesn't look up.

"You never know. I might be fascinated. Why the reticence? Are you an assassin or something?"

He snorts. "I'm a stunt coordinator."

I do a double take. "Bullshit! You're winding me up. Get out of here! A stuntman? You are not!"

He shrugs and smiles ruefully. "Afraid so."

I have to admit —as I sit up in my seat and pay a bit more attention to his penetrating gray eyes, cashmere gray jumper and jean-clad thighs noting everything about him is understated, I decide he does kind of look as if he might be in great physical shape.

"Hmm! But you don't actually do the stunts yourself? You coordinate them."

He opens his book again. "I wouldn't ask anyone to do something I wasn't prepared to do myself. I test the stunts out first. Often I end up doing them."

"I'm...actually...surprised." I shake my head. Seriously? As well as being somewhat understated, he's got this nerdy vibe going on, what with the reading glasses and all. "So, while the rest of us were crapping our pants, just now, you were like, this is just another day's work at the office..."

The upper lip twitches. "Not exactly. I don't like the unexpected any more than the next person."

I fold my arms and give him a slight nudge. "Go on. Tell me more. I'm intrigued."

❄

If you'd like to read the rest of the story, you can grab your copy here!

NEW BOOK ON ITS WAY

For fans of close proximity, fake dates and holiday romances...

After 'Alice in Wanderlust', escape with this roadtrip romcom 'Alice and the Impossible Game'.

AFTERWORD

HAPPY HOLIDAYS!

Anna Foxkirk is an award-winning author of romcom, fantasy and historical fiction. Her first novella, *Alice in Wanderlust*, was published in November 2020, and in the same year she was voted Favorite Debut Romance Author of 2020 by the Australian Romance Readers Association.

The best way to hear my latest news is through my Foxtrot newsletter in which I share not only what I'm up to, but also other author interviews and some exciting giveaways. Join me here: https://annafoxkirk.substack.com

If you'd like to check out my website, here's that link:
https://www.annafoxkirk.com
And finally, you'll also find me on Instagram:
https://www.instagram.com/annafoxkirk/

A final note…

I hope you enjoyed *Be My Valerie*. If you did and would like to make my 'happy ever after', please leave a short review. It doesn't need to be long, but your feedback is invaluable to me as an author and helps other readers find my fiction. I'd love you to help spread the word.

Before you go, let me wish you all the very best for the year ahead. I hope you read what you love and love what you read!

Warm wishes,

Anna

Printed in Great Britain
by Amazon